CAMPFIRE STORIES

FROM COAST TO COAST

CAMPFIRE STORIES

FROM COAST TO COAST

Barbara Smith

Heritage House Publishing Company Ltd.
heritagehouse.ca

Cataloguing information available from Library and Archives Canada

978-1-77203-311-3 (pbk)
978-1-77203-312-0 (ebook)

Edited by Karla Decker
Proofread by Lesley Cameron
Cover and interior book design by Jacqui Thomas

The interior of this book was produced on 100% post-consumer recycled paper, processed chlorine free, and printed with vegetable based inks.

Heritage House gratefully acknowledges that the land on which we live and work is within the traditional territories of the Lkwungen (Esquimalt and Songhees), Malahat, Pacheedaht, Scia'new, T'Sou-ke, and W̱SÁNEĆ (Pauquachin, Tsartlip, Tsawout, Tseycum) Peoples.

We acknowledge the financial support of the Government of Canada through the Canada Book Fund (CBF) and the Canada Council for the Arts, and the Province of British Columbia through the British Columbia Arts Council and the Book Publishing Tax Credit.

24 23 22 21 20   1 2 3 4 5

Printed in Canada

For Bob, Debbie, and Robyn: ⟶

**From beginning to end,
I can't imagine my world without you in it.**

CONTENTS

INTRODUCTION

Greetings to you, all my happy campers from coast to coast to coast—or should that be from ghost to ghost to ghost?

I hope you're ready to enjoy the delicious shiver of a campfire story or two while you're huddled around a bonfire with your friends and family. Or, if you dare, you can read the stories in this book while you're alone in bed, tucked under the covers, with only a flashlight for company.

Don't worry about getting too scared, because, after all, these stories are just made up, right? Wrong! Some of the tales in this book are based on true stories. If you're curious about which ones those are, just check the afterword—which, logically, is at the back of the book.

In the meantime, settle in to enjoy some scary tales—and please—pass the s'mores!

TIPS FOR STORYTELLERS

1. If you're going to be reading a story aloud, try to be as relaxed as possible. Make sure you've read the story over a few times first so that you know the material. Remember, your audience is eager to hear what you're about to tell or read. Think of yourself as telling a story to a friend.

2. Select a story that's appropriate for your group. You can always inject an extra shot of creepy by adapting the setting to a place close to home.

3. Even if it's not camping season, you can create an eerie atmosphere with candlelight. Make sure everyone's turned off their phones!

4. Glance up from the book to make eye contact with your audience periodically, and don't forget to pause and lower your voice occasionally for a dramatic effect.

5. Don't draw the story out past its natural conclusion. A good campfire story requires an effective ending. Be sure

to follow that ending with a moment of silence to let your listeners absorb the story.

6. Enjoy the experience! Being deliciously frightened is so much fun!

STORIES BY FIRELIGHT

NIGHT TERROR

On a muggy evening in August, Carly was heading out of Halifax to join her family on a camping trip at the shore. She was looking forward to seeing everyone, but she was also a bit nervous because this was the first time she'd ever made the drive alone.

She turned on the radio for some company. *Being alone has its advantages,* she thought. *I can sing along with the tunes, and no one will complain about my awful singing voice.* She tuned the dial to a station that she knew played music she liked. At the moment, though, there was no music, just news.

The radio announcer's voice was low and calm, but his message was alarming. "We have been asked to advise people that there has been an escape from the local prison. One man is still on the loose. He is known to prey on young women who are alone. Please, everyone, be vigilant."

Carly locked her car doors but kept driving, feeling completely safe. She was no child. She knew how to take care of herself and keep herself out of harm's way. Even so, the announcer's words lingered in her mind.

Once she was out of the city limits, Carly pulled into a service station. She needed to top up the gas tank, check the oil, and use the restroom. The sky had darkened as she'd been driving, and she recognized that sharpness in the air that meant a thunderstorm was brewing. Carly knew the sky would be overcast for the rest of her drive, but she hoped she could get to the campground before the storm started.

She filled the gas tank and made quick use of the station's dingy little restroom. The cracked mirror above the sink distorted her appearance, as though someone had taken a knife and slashed through her face. Carly shuddered as she walked toward the gas bar to pay her bill. The clerk standing behind the cash register gave her a friendly smile.

"Looks like it's going to be a nasty night," he commented as he pointed a grimy finger at the signs outside whipping in the wind.

Carly nodded silently and looked around the small, shabby room. Her confidence was starting to flake away. The clerk might have been a decent guy, but she had no way of knowing that for certain because he was a stranger to her and, of course, she had always been warned about "stranger danger." She took the coins he gave her in change and then hurried out the door toward the safety of her car.

She was almost there when she heard the bells on the door jangle behind her.

"Wait!" the man called to her.

But Carly didn't wait. Instead, she hurried the last few steps.

"I'm in a rush!" she called out to him as she reached the door on the driver's side of her car. She pulled the door handle up, jumped into the car, and locked it. Only then did she dare to look up. When she did, she saw the attendant standing by her car.

When she'd seen him inside, he had looked grubby and dishevelled. She'd chalked that up to being the appearance of a man who worked in a gas station, but now that he was outside, under the artificial brightness of fluorescent lights, the man had taken on a more threatening appearance. His face was pale and unshaven, and his eyes were sunk back in their sockets and darting wildly to and fro.

"I made a mistake," he said to Carly as he quickly walked toward her. Now, even his voice sounded different, more urgent. He really didn't want her to get away.

"I gave you the wrong change. Come back inside. It'll only take a minute."

Carly could feel her pulse drumming in her ears. *He's no service station attendant*, she thought. *This man's the escaped convict!*

"No!" she yelled through the closed window. "I don't care about my change!" She turned the key in the ignition and breathed a sigh of relief as the engine roared to life.

But when she looked up again, the man was still right beside her window.

"No, don't go. It's you who owes me money," he said as he waved his arms frantically. "You have to come back inside with me."

Carly eased her foot down on the gas pedal and steered toward the road, but the crazy man ran to the front of her car, blocking her way. That scared her. She couldn't allow him to trap her. She rifled around the bottom of her purse, opened the car window a few centimetres, and threw a handful of coins on the ground before screaming to the man, "That's more than enough! Now get out of my way!"

But the man wouldn't budge. He placed his hands on the hood of the car and looked directly into Carly's eyes. Slowly, he shook his head. Silently, he mouthed the word "No."

Terrified, Carly jolted into action. She put the car in gear and stepped hard on the gas pedal. The man jumped out of the way but barely made it in time. The front fender of the car still managed to brush his thigh, knocking him to the pavement.

I'm safe now, Carly thought, wiping sweat from her face. She pulled onto the highway, spraying gravel in her wake. Once the car's tires got traction, she risked a quick look back. To her horror, she saw the station attendant running to a pickup truck parked in the stall marked EMPLOYEES.

Carly pressed her foot harder on the gas pedal, pushing the car to its limit. *I've got to get away from him.* But the best the car could give wasn't good enough. Headlights from the man's pickup truck loomed behind her. He flashed his headlights to high beam time and time again and blasted his horn insistently.

Oh my God! Carly thought. *He's trying to drive me off the road!*

The truck pulled up so close behind her that she was terrified he was going to ram her car. Its horn blared with deafening persistence. Then, thankfully, the driver backed off slightly and, for a moment, Carly relaxed a bit.

But then he blasted her with his bright lights again, flicking them on and off, intermittently flooding her car with harsh light and blinding her when she dared to glance in the rearview mirror. It was nearly impossible to keep her car on the road under these conditions. Sour bile rose up in Carly's throat. She not only feared the maniac chasing her, but she feared herself, too. Her concentration had been washed away by panic. It would only be a matter of time before she missed one of the turns on the darkened highway.

The life-threatening game of cat-and-mouse continued until they were close to the campground. When Carly saw the familiar gravel driveway, she cranked hard on the steering wheel, turning the car as fast and sharply as she could. For a moment she thought the car would flip over, but she managed to regain control at the last minute and then slammed on the brakes. She threw open her door and made a dash to the campground office, all the while screaming for help.

When she reached the small building, she screamed, "Call the police now!" She turned and pointed to the truck, which was stopped right behind her car. The driver had stepped out of his vehicle and was moving toward her, slowly, menacingly. Then she saw a flash of metal in his right hand. He was armed.

Campground security arrived before the police did, but there were enough of them that the truck driver knew he was well outnumbered. He threw his gun down on the ground and yelled, "I've been trying to protect her! There's a man in the back seat of that woman's car—with a knife!"

He was telling the truth. There, crouched in the shadows of her car's back seat, was an enormous man with a deadly glint in his eye. When he saw Carly looking at him, he grinned broadly and waved a large knife at her.

A moment later, the police arrived. Finally, Carly was safe. They pulled the man out of her car, handcuffed him, and locked him in the back of one of their cruisers.

One constable approached the truck driver and asked him why he hadn't just phoned the police when he saw the man get into Carly's car. He explained that he was afraid to take his eyes off the madman for even a moment and that he was sure Carly would've been dead by now if he had.

"Why were you flashing your bright lights at me like that?" Carly asked the man.

"Every time I did that, the guy was starting to reach up and over for you with his knife. Whenever I flashed my lights, I could see him, and he backed down. I guess he realized I would be able to recognize him."

By this time, Carly's parents were at her side. "We're so thankful that truck driver saved you," her mother said as she hugged Carly tight.

But for Carly, it took a while to think of the man she thought was trying to kill her as her rescuer. Once she did, though, she thanked him many times over.

And she never again got into her car without checking to make sure that the back seat was empty.

THE CABIN

Jeff and Sue wanted to buy a cabin in the woods. They both worked at high-pressure jobs in Winnipeg, so having a quiet getaway spot would provide them with a place to relax and reconnect with each other.

On the May long weekend, Jeff suggested that they pack a lunch and head out into the beautiful Manitoba countryside.

"We don't have to be back to work until Tuesday morning. We can even get a motel room and stay away for a couple of nights," he added.

"Sounds great," Sue said enthusiastically. "If we find a cabin this weekend, we can enjoy it this summer!"

An hour later, the two were headed west and ready for an adventure. As they drove, they talked about the pros and cons of buying a fixer-upper or one that was move-in ready.

"We don't want to spend too much," Jeff cautioned, but even as he spoke, Sue could see the hint of a smile forming at the edges of her husband's lips. They both knew how important this purchase was to their future, a place where they could go, year after year, to escape the cares of city life.

As they drove along the back roads, the sun shone and the trip seemed full of promise. Sue drove slowly, and both of them scanned the countryside in search of real-estate signs. But there were none to be seen.

Just as they were about to give up and turn the car around, Jeff pointed to what looked like a driveway at the side of the road. A dilapidated-looking FOR SALE sign lay at an angle near an old fence post.

"That sign looks pretty old," Sue said. "Maybe the place sold ages ago and the new owners just forgot to take down the sign."

"We're here now. Let's check it out," said Jeff.

Sue steered the car off the narrow road on to an even narrower lane.

"You could barely call this a driveway," she said, her foot resting on the brake pedal. "It's not much more than two ruts cut into an evergreen forest."

"Maybe we shouldn't bother," Jeff said, trying to keep from sounding as nervous as he was beginning to feel.

"We're committed now. There's no place to turn the car around."

Towering pine trees blocked the sun, their branches scraping against the car windows like green fingernails. Jeff reached over and put his hand on Sue's arm. "This isn't a good idea, Sue. Stop here. There can't be anything up ahead, and besides, the car's getting scratch marks all over it."

Sue nodded glumly before stopping the car. She looked down and moved the gearshift lever into reverse. When she looked up again, she could hardly believe her eyes. There, not three metres away, was a clearing. The sun shone brightly, and there was lots of space to turn the car around.

"Would you look at that!" Sue exclaimed.

"What a relief," Jeff said with a sigh. "We'll be out of here in no time."

"Wait," Sue replied. "Look! There's an old cabin at the back edge of the clearing."

Excitement had suddenly replaced the unease Sue had been feeling. She jumped out of the car, signalling for Jeff to follow her. Sure enough, her eyes had not deceived her. An old, abandoned house stood on the property, sheltered by a semi-circle of tall pine trees. Its clapboard siding had weathered to grey and a few of the windows were broken, but even so, there was no denying that they had stumbled upon a cabin in the woods, which was, after all, what they had been searching for.

Sue slowed her pace as she approached the old house. "Hurry," she urged Jeff. "I'm not going in there without you."

Jeff grasped Sue's shoulders. "Don't try to go in," he warned. "That front door looks as though it's ready to fall off."

"We're here now. It would be a shame not to investigate," Sue said. "Besides, it's certainly a fixer-upper, like we talked about. The place is bound to be a bargain, and we can renovate it."

Jeff scuffed the toe of his right shoe into the dust. "Rebuild, you mean. That's no renovation project. I don't think we could handle it. Besides, there's something creepy about this place. We should get out of here."

"Let's just take one peek inside," Sue pleaded, grabbing Jeff's hand and leading the way through knee-high weeds up to the cabin.

As she pulled on the door, its one remaining hinge creaked in protest.

"You see? The place doesn't want us here," he said. "And besides, we're trespassing."

Sue wanted to tell her husband not to be a nervous old lady, but she had to admit to herself that something about the place did creep her out. She took a deep breath and stepped across the threshold before stopping dead in her tracks, choking on the dust-filled air. Jeff brushed cobwebs from his face and hair as he resisted a strong impulse to turn around and run back to the car.

Inside, the cabin was dark and cold, as if sunshine hadn't brightened or warmed the place for years. But once Sue's and Jeff's eyes adjusted to the darkness, they could see that the run-down old place was still furnished. There were even dishes set on the table and tufts of curtains hanging on the grimy windows. An old-fashioned coffee percolator sat on the stove, and faded cushions lay on a broken-down couch.

Sue whispered, "It's as if the people who lived here just picked up and left."

"About a hundred years ago," Jeff whispered back.

As they spoke, a slight movement in the corner of the room caught their attention. Was that a shadow? How could that be? There wasn't enough light to cast a shadow. But it was a shadow, and it was thickening as they watched. Then another shadow appeared beside the first one. As Jeff and Sue stared, the shapes lengthened and darkened until the slightly blurry images of two people stared back at them.

Sue shook her head and looked around. When she looked back, the shadow people were still there, now clear enough that she could make out some details. The pair appeared to be young, but they were dressed in clothes from the 1950s. Their eyes stared sightlessly, devoid of life.

"We didn't mean to disturb you," Jeff told the apparitions, his voice shaking.

With that, he reached for Sue's hand, and together they ran back to the car. It was several minutes before she was calm enough to even start the car, let alone drive. But once they had calmed their breathing, the pair drove away as fast as they dared and didn't stop until they'd reached the nearest town, where they went into the first coffee shop they came to.

Still shaking, they each ordered bowls of chili, hoping that some comfort food would help calm their nerves. When the server brought their meals, she welcomed them to town. "I haven't seen you here before, so I figure you must be visiting. What brought you out this way?"

Jeff cleared his throat before he spoke. "We're looking to buy a cabin or a cottage."

"Don't know of any for sale around here. Well, unless you count the old Allen place down the road a bit, but I doubt that you'd be interested in that one. It's been for sale since long before I was born."

"The Allen place?" Sue inquired tentatively.

The young woman nodded.

"Chuck and Arlene Allen have become part of the local history around here. Their old cabin's still standing, as far as I know. Legend has it that they died within a few days of one another and their place has stood empty ever since. Of course, every generation of teenagers claims that the cabin's haunted, and who knows, maybe it is. I'll leave you to enjoy your chili now," the server said as she set the steaming bowls down before them.

"Oh, yes," Sue whispered to Jeff. "The old Allen place is haunted all right. No one knows better than we do that it's well and truly haunted."

CAPTURED

Bert was a solitary kind of guy and a real outdoorsman. He loved nothing more than being alone in the beautiful back-country of British Columbia. And so it was that, one summer, Bert was camping near Toba Inlet on BC's rugged coast. He'd heard a rumour about gold veins running through the creeks and rivers near there, and he thought he'd snoop around a bit to see what he could find.

He didn't find any gold on the first day, but he did get a good feel for the area and was well satisfied by the time he crawled into his sleeping bag that night. The next morning, he woke up feeling refreshed after a good night's sleep under the stars and set out for another day's prospecting. Once again, he headed back to his campsite empty-handed, but that didn't bother him. Sure, he'd love to strike a rich vein, but he was happy enough just being on his own in the wilds—until, that is, he reached his campsite that evening and found the place in ruins. Someone or something had strewn his belongings all over the place. When he took a closer look, he couldn't see that anything was missing, so he figured the intruder wasn't a human but an animal, a good-sized one, maybe a bear or a wolf.

Bert straightened the mess, then fried himself a fish he'd caught and shortly afterward climbed into his sleeping bag for the night. This time, though, he kept his rifle close at hand. If the varmint that messed with his gear came back, he would be ready to take revenge.

Several hours later, Bert was in a deep sleep when he felt himself being lifted up to a great height, sleeping bag and all. Something had picked him up and was carrying him in his sleeping bag, like Santa Claus carrying a sackful of toys. Panicked, Bert screamed and kicked and punched his captor, but to no avail. Whatever had him just kept on moving and at a good pace, too. Bert's body was slammed against whatever it was with every step it took.

After several more hours, the movement finally stopped and the kidnapper dumped Bert onto the ground in a heap. The poor man was exhausted from his attempts to get free, and every part of his body was badly bruised. He lay where he'd been dropped, hiding in his sleeping bag and falling in and out of consciousness, too sore to even try to sit up, let alone try to escape. All the while, he heard thunderous grunts, ear-splitting yowls, and mysterious chattering. By nightfall, all was quiet.

When the sun rose the next morning, Bert eased himself up on his elbow. His body was sore, but he didn't think any of his bones were broken. He looked around and saw that he had been carried into a deep valley with a narrow opening at the far end. Just at the opening, four enormous, hairy creatures huddled together. Fear shot through Bert's body. He could barely breathe. He knew the Indigenous legends about giant sasquatches, but he'd never put much stock in such stories.

Now he wondered if maybe he should have. He called out to the enormous creatures, who roared back at him in response.

What to do? The beasts were blocking the only path from the valley but, even if they weren't, Bert had no idea where he was and therefore no idea of where to go to find help.

He could see that whichever beast had carried him away had also brought his knapsack and dropped it next to him, so at least he had rations to last him for a few days. He set up a rudimentary campsite with the materials he had and kept his distance from the strange creatures.

Over the next few days, Bert watched the beasts carefully. He came to regard the group as a family—a mother, a father, a daughter, and a son. He was heartened to see that they interacted amiably. This gave him confidence and, when the creatures were distracted, Bert edged himself and his belongings closer and closer to the opening of the valley, hoping to escape as the monsters slept.

He had almost succeeded, but the enormous father must have sensed him approaching. The creature jumped to its feet and waved its arms threateningly. Bert had a rifle and a handful of bullets, but they did no good against this huge animal, who was solidly built and at least three metres tall.

The large female was nearly as big but much more docile. The two younger ones seemed to be afraid of Bert, so he tried to show them that he wasn't a threat; having them as allies might help him escape. He searched through his belongings and found a pack of tobacco. Bert held it out toward the young male, who dipped his finger inside and then licked his hand. The taste seemed to appeal to him, and this attracted the father, who grabbed the package and poured its contents into his mouth.

The beast's reaction to the tobacco was swift and dramatic. Its body began to twitch and shudder. Then, taking gigantic leaps, it ran for a nearby stream and hurled itself in. The female and the two young followed. Bert knew this might well be his only opportunity to flee from his captors. He ran until he couldn't run anymore. He looked behind and didn't see the creatures following him. Relieved, he hid in a bush and slept for the night.

The next morning, Bert headed out again and was lucky enough to encounter a crew of lumberjacks. His relief was overwhelming. He dropped to his knees and silently thanked every deity he could think of before calling out, "Hey, fellas, I'm lost. Could you give me directions to the nearest town?"

Then, because Bert was Canadian, he added, "please."

LITTLE GIRL LOST

Frank Duncan and Harry Scott were trappers who lived in Rankin Inlet, Nunavut, on the west coast of Hudson Bay. One summer day, they had been out with their dogs checking traplines when the weather turned bad: a storm moved in, and rain pelted down in fat drops pushed by the sharp edge of a fierce wind. The temperature dropped rapidly, and they knew they had to find shelter, or they and the dogs might not make it through the night.

Harry thought he remembered there being an old shack not too far away, and so, fighting the wind, they headed in that direction. Their visibility through the curtain of rain was nearly zero, but they encouraged each other with words they didn't really believe, and eventually they reached the comparative safety of a rundown old cabin. There were gaping holes between the logs, which meant the place didn't offer much protection, but at least they had a roof over their heads.

Frank built a fire and cooked what little grub they had, and they shared it with the dogs. They hunkered down for the night as best they could, and both men were fast asleep when they were wakened by the dogs whimpering and yelping outside.

"What's wrong with them?" Frank asked as he hurried to join Harry, who was already outside the cabin.

All was quiet—except for the dogs, who were tugging at their leads in what looked like spasms of terror. The men tried to calm the animals, but no matter what they did or said, the dogs would not settle down. Finally, Harry suggested that they would have to bring the animals into the cabin with them. Frank agreed.

But, as they turned toward the cabin door, they saw a sight that neither one would ever forget. A child, a little girl, wearing only a light cotton dress stood before them. She was sobbing her heart out. Harry and Frank looked at one another. This wasn't possible.

When they looked her way again, she had vanished.

But that wasn't possible either.

They had both seen her. Frantically, the two searched around the cabin. The dogs were still barking and growling.

"We need to go for help," Frank said. Leaving their make-shift camp, they took the dogs and made for town as fast as they could go. They burst into the RCMP station, shouting that they needed help to find the little girl they'd seen.

"If we don't get to her quickly, she could die out there!" Harry shouted.

"Settle down a minute, there," the officer said with a bored look on his face.

"No, we won't settle down," Frank insisted. "There's a child out there who's in grave danger."

The officer rubbed his eyes with the back of his hand. "There's no child out there in danger or otherwise. What you saw was a ghost."

"There's no such thing as a ghost," Harry retorted.

"Sorry to tell you, boys, but apparently there is such a thing as a ghost, and the ghost of a little girl haunts that old abandoned trapper's cabin."

Frank and Harry both opened their mouths to disagree and try to impress on this foolish policeman that a girl's life was on the line, but the officer held up his hand to silence them.

"This detachment has records going back forty years about that ghost. I've never seen her myself, but I've heard that an encounter with her leaves a person pretty upset."

Frank drew in a big breath, and Harry leaned against the desk. What they were hearing was as unbelievable as what they had seen.

The RCMP officer continued, "The way I've been told, the girl was one of ten kids. Her family was boarding a ship to leave the Inlet. Somehow one of the daughters was left behind, probably at their homestead. They didn't notice her missing until they were bunked down in the ship. By then, they were a good way out into the bay, and a nasty rainstorm and a driving wind had picked up. It took the captain of the ship another day to get the craft back to shore. And by then, it was too late. They couldn't find their daughter anywhere. It's said she only appears during windstorms."

Frank and Harry were barely breathing by the time the policeman was finished telling them about the ghostly legend.

"Poor wee thing," Frank said quietly.

"From the looks of her, she might have died of fright," Harry added.

When the weather calmed, the two men went back to the old cabin and laid a stone at the spot where they had seen the tiny spectre so that she would know she hadn't been forgotten.

It's said that since the men's heartfelt gesture was made, there haven't been any sightings of the ghostly girl, not even in violent windstorms. Perhaps, thanks to their thoughtfulness, her soul now rests in peace—through any kind of storm.

CEMETERY WALK

Most of the people who knew Raj thought he was weird—even Raj occasionally wondered about himself, especially his strange hobbies. For one thing, he was a big-time *Star Trek* fan. He pretty much structured his life around Trekkie conventions. His favourite was the one held in the small southeastern town of Vulcan, Alberta, a place that capitalized on the coincidence of sharing a name with the birthplace of one of the show's popular characters, Spock.

But *Star Trek* wasn't all that intrigued Raj. He was fascinated by almost anything paranormal. He was intrigued by the possibility that somewhere in the rugged vastness of the Rocky Mountains, at least one sasquatch family lumbered about, hidden from the prying eyes of civilization. He also thought that a monster might really live in Okanagan Lake, and that UFOs toured the Milky Way.

Raj's view of reality hadn't made life easy for him. Over the years, he'd taken lots of mean-spirited teasing about his beliefs, and by this point in his life, he only felt included and safe from criticism when he was with other self-professed paranormal geeks.

Unfortunately, empathy didn't run very thick in Raj's veins, and he took advantage of those rare occasions when he did feel comfortable by making cruel fun of anyone who expressed a belief in the one feature of the supernatural that he didn't subscribe to—ghosts. He liked to give the impression that only folks who weren't too bright would have any interest in the spirit world. He'd managed to hurt a lot of people's feelings that way, but, in his warped assessment, this somehow evened the score with the people who had teased him and thus justified his own cruelty.

In reality, however, there was an entirely different reason for his mocking. Raj was utterly terrified by the very idea that a disembodied soul could somehow roam the earth. His fear was so great that he didn't even like to hear about ghosts and he always did his best to avoid being near a cemetery. Sometimes, he would even pass up a potentially terrific paranormal conference just because the topic of ghosts was on the agenda. Other times, though, the temptation to attend, even if ghosts were going to be discussed, was just too great, and this was the case one particular summer when an outdoor event was held in southern Saskatchewan. Everyone was camping, and the featured events took place in a large tent so that expenses could be kept low. The atmosphere was casual. He'd traded information with other Trekkies, listened to an expert on crop circles, and even spent what he considered to be quality time heckling a speaker who had written a book of supposedly true ghost stories.

At the end of the weekend, as he headed for home on a deserted rural road, Raj was a happy camper, so happy that he hadn't remembered to fill his old beater of a car with gas before he'd set out. It wasn't until the car lurched to a stop that he realized his mistake.

What to do? The sun was already setting, and he didn't want to be stranded at night in the middle of the narrow road. The only option was to start walking. He'd be sure to come to a farmhouse not too far away, he thought to himself as he set out with uncharacteristic optimism.

But forty-five minutes later, with inky darkness closing in on him, Raj's hopeful mood had deteriorated to serious apprehension. Worse, he was so tired and thirsty that he really didn't think he'd make it back to his car. Again he wondered, what to do? Plan A certainly hadn't worked out well.

A nap at the side of the road? Well, only if he really had to. What about the opposite? Some jumping jacks and running on the spot to revive him might do the trick.

It worked! The exercise perked him up! He gave his arms a final stretch and started walking again. Soon he could see a light shining in the distance. His determination had paid off. The light had to be coming from someone's house. Maybe he'd found the help he needed. Now, he just needed to get to that help, as quickly as possible. The shortest route was a straight line, diagonally across a field. Yes, that would work.

Raj had only taken one step when he realized that it was not a field in front of him. It was a cemetery.

A massive shiver ran through his body, and he heard himself whimper. Mind over matter, he reminded himself, and, keeping his eyes trained on the light up ahead, he took another tentative step off the road.

"Keep focused." Raj knew he was standing still and talking to himself, but somehow it helped. "Keep your eyes on the prize, and that prize is the light on the other side of this stupid cemetery. Besides, the speaker this afternoon had even said that graveyards weren't often haunted—not that there really was such a thing as ghosts anyway."

With his mind made up, his body followed—unfortunately, into a puddle at the side of the road. By the time he had scrambled to his feet again, he not only was scared, tired, and soaking wet, but also had realized that he simply had no choice. He would have to pull himself over the rotting plank fence that surrounded the cemetery and then walk between the graves.

He climbed over the fence and lowered himself onto the cemetery grass. With each step he took, his wet sneakers made gurgling noises that sounded disturbingly like someone was being choked.

Huge granite markers and spindly trees marked the graves where he fervently hoped the dearly departed lay in complete peace. A line of cedar trees moaned and sighed as a gust of wind blew through the cemetery. Raj whimpered in fear. Tears coursed down his face.

"I can't do this," he told himself. "I'm too scared. I might as well give up. I'm gonna end up in a cemetery anyway. It might as well be this one, and it might as well be tonight. I just hope I haven't disturbed any souls already resting here."

Defeated, Raj felt his knees giving out. He looked up one last time—and found himself face-to-face with a beautiful young woman. He screamed in fright and slammed his hands against his chest.

"Oh, dear God, you scared me," he said, rather unnecessarily. "What on earth are you doing here?"

"Oh, I walk here frequently," the pretty girl replied with a smile warm enough to make Raj realize, with embarrassment, that he'd been rude. He had probably scared her at least as much as she scared him. He should have explained his own presence there in the cemetery before asking questions of a stranger.

He tried to speak in a more reasonable tone. "My car ran out of gas, and I'm trying to get to that house over there, the one with the light on inside. But I'm scared because I've never walked through a cemetery before."

"I was scared, too, when I first got here, but by now it just feels like home," the woman answered—before vanishing into a column of mist.

It took a moment for the reality of his surreal situation to register with Raj. When it did, he fainted dead away.

THE HOUSE THAT HATED

The first time Vik and Anu saw the old place, something about it made them both fall in love with it. And that "something" certainly wasn't its graceful appearance, because this house was one ugly duckling. But the location—ahh, the location—in the picturesque countryside of Prince Edward Island was perfect. The driveway behind led to the main road, and the front windows framed a beautiful view of the water. Best of all, the price was right.

When the couple contacted their real-estate company, they were told that the cottage was well over a hundred years old and that it had originally been built as an inn for thirsty, weary travellers. That appealed to Anu's sense of whimsy and to Vik's love of history, so they wasted no time in using all of their combined savings to buy the place and declare it to be their first-ever home.

They moved in with only the bare essentials, knowing that they had weeks of hard work ahead of them. Fortunately, those essentials included a washer and a dryer that two delivery-men inched down the ladder-like steps into the cellar. Doing frequent loads of laundry would be a necessity while they worked on the house, so those machines would get a good workout.

For the first month that the young couple lived there, they were so exhausted each night that they crawled into bed and fell asleep immediately. Finally, after weeks of effort, their new home was starting to look the way they wanted it to, and so they decided they deserved a day off.

First, they took a carafe of coffee outside and sat enjoying the view of the crystal-clear lake. Inevitably, though, they began chatting about the house.

"Have you had a good look around the cellar?" Vik asked.

"Of course, I've been doing laundry down there twice a week," Anu replied. "It's pretty awful, eh?"

Vik nodded. "It's so dark down there that I never noticed that one wall's all blackened. It looks as though there was a fire."

"I think you're right. Well, at least it proves that the foundation can stand up to the elements," Anu responded, trying to put a positive spin on the huge, hideous scorch mark covering the wall behind the old-fashioned furnace.

"Let's drive into town," suggested Vik. "We can poke around the shops and grab some lunch too."

Anu nodded enthusiastically, and soon they were on the road into town. After several hours of window-shopping, browsing through a well-stocked bookstore, and eating delicious turkey club sandwiches, Anu predicted that they would be happy forever in their house near this lovely little town. They drove home completely content, not knowing just how dreadfully wrong that optimistic prediction was.

As they stepped inside the house, they both recoiled and their hands flew to their faces.

"What is that smell?" Vik asked.

Anu could only shake her head. She had one hand over her mouth and nose, and her eyes watered from the stinging, acrid odour.

As they slowly walked inside, the awful stench grew stronger and stronger with each step. Yet, the rooms looked exactly as they had when they left.

"What cleaner did you use? It smells awful," Vik said.

"Nothing different. Just the stuff I always use." Anu soaked a dishtowel in cold water and held it over her nose and mouth.

They peered into the living room. There, in the corner of the window, a thick, black cobweb had entwined itself around the handle that opened the window. The stench radiated from its thick tendrils.

"If that's a spider's web, then we clearly have an infestation of huge spiders."

"Huge and stinky beyond belief," Anu added. "But I've never once seen a spider in this house."

Vik nodded in agreement. "I've never seen any sort of bug in the house."

"Standing here's not helping. Grab the work gloves and we'll tackle this."

But the solution wasn't as straightforward as it seemed. The malodorous web had a gooey consistency that resisted their efforts to remove it, and they had to hold their breath while they scrubbed, each running outside for fresh air every few minutes. Finally, using paint scrapers, they managed to remove the ugly, smelly web.

"It's good that we're finished scraping off old paint, because these scrapers have to go into the garbage," Vik said as they worked to get themselves and their equipment cleaned up after the nightmarish chore.

They fell into bed exhausted again that night, but now they no longer felt as happy or as settled as they had the previous nights.

In the middle of the night, Vik bolted upright in bed, grasping at his throat and coughing.

"There's no air in here," he gasped as he shook Anu awake.

They ran outside and stood inhaling deep gulps of fresh air until they could breathe easily again.

"It's the trees," Vik suggested. "They're too close to the house."

"But those willows are gorgeous, and trees are supposed to create oxygen, not take it away."

"Well, the trees are going to have to go. We can't live like this." It was clear to Anu that he had made up his mind. She was going to have to play this one carefully, because she really didn't want to lose those weeping willows.

"My brother said he'd come for a visit soon. Let's wait till then. If we have to cut them down, he can help," Anu suggested, hoping that she could at least delay the destruction.

Tentatively, they went back into the house. The air inside was fine. The cloying thickness was gone.

"How can that be?" Vik asked, his frustration audible.

Anu shook her head. "We should go back to bed, at least for a couple more hours."

Early the next morning, Vik heard Anu sigh in her sleep. Thinking she was having a nightmare, he turned to comfort her, but her side of the bed was empty.

"Where are you?" he called.

"In the kitchen. Want some coffee?" she called back.

Before Vik could answer, he heard another sigh. It came from inside the wall. He held his breath to hear more clearly, but all was silent.

"Yeah, sure. I'll be right there," he said as he put on his slippers. He'd no sooner stood up than he heard the sigh again. But this time it was more than a sigh. It was a sob, as though someone was sobbing their heart out.

"You okay, Anu?"

"I'm fine. Your coffee's poured. Let's have it outside again this morning."

Neither of them mentioned the recent strange incidents.

Later in the day, as Vik worked in the shop attached to the house, he heard footsteps pounding across the attic floor. Why would Anu be up in the attic, he wondered. But when he looked away from his workbench, he saw that his wife was in the next room, wiping the dining room table. He shook his head and continued with the task at hand.

By evening, both of them were tired and irritable. Knowing that a good night's sleep would help, they went to bed early.

An hour later, Anu woke up gagging from the stench that had permeated the house a few days before. She got out of bed as quietly as she could and went into the living room and over to the window. There, tangled in the slats of the blinds, was another black, sticky web. Feeling utterly defeated, she sat on the floor, ignoring the stench pouring over her in waves.

When she heard footsteps from the floor above, she smiled with relief. At least Vik was awake. She'd wait for him to come downstairs, and then they could talk this over. When he hadn't appeared after fifteen minutes, she went looking for him—and found him still fast asleep in bed. Who had been walking around upstairs?

Vik was in such a good mood when he finally did come into the kitchen that Anu decided not to mention the footsteps she'd heard. After all, her brother was coming to spend the weekend and he brought fun with him wherever he went. *Maybe that's all we need*, she thought, *a bit of vibrancy in the house*. She'd do some laundry to make sure the sheets and towels were fresh for their guest.

But as she climbed down the precarious steps to the cellar, the air became thicker and thicker, until she was choking with each breath. Determined to finish her chores, Anu put the laundry basket down on the floor in front of the washer. She turned to reach for the detergent.

And then she screamed.

A thick, black pulsating cobweb covered the scorched cinderblock wall. She dropped the detergent and climbed up the rickety stairs as quickly as she could.

There stood her brother. "Such a rush just to see your baby brother?"

"Oh, Sam," Anu said as she fell into his arms, babbling about their strange experiences in the house. Vik overheard the excited chatter and came in from the shop.

"What she's saying is true, Sam. It's been terrible here. We need some help, or we can't stay here."

This was the first time either Vik or Anu had acknowledged exactly how bad their lives had been since they'd moved into the old house.

"You're sure it's not your imaginations working overtime?" Sam asked.

Anu grabbed her brother's hand. "Come downstairs with me. I'll show you the web on the wall. I swear it was moving, pulsing, as if some current was flowing through it."

But when the siblings reached the bottom step, the scorched wall appeared to be just that—a scorched cinderblock wall. There were no webs, pulsing or otherwise, anywhere in the basement. Sam's suggestion seemed to be confirmed, and so the three settled in to spend a companionable evening talking over old times and bringing each other up to date on their busy lives. It was after twelve by the time they all went off to bed. They'd deal with any problems in the morning, if there really were any problems.

But morning didn't come soon enough for any one of the three people in that house. Vik and Anu were awakened by Sam screaming for help. They found him in the hallway, clawing at his face. A web had wrapped itself completely around his head. Anu turned on the nearest light and held tightly onto her brother while Vik brushed the thick membranes from around Sam's head.

By now they knew for certain that some sort of unnatural being inhabited this house. They also knew that whatever it was, it had taken its game up one notch too far. Sam explained that he'd been awakened by the sound of a sorrowful sobbing. "Then a voice began calling my name—over and over and over again."

Vik and Anu realized that they had no choice. Despite the hours of work they had put into the house, they would have to sell it as soon as possible. It was clear that the house they had loved did not love them back. They went into the living room to tell Sam their decision. They had no sooner set foot in the room than a small fire flared to life under the window. The fire extinguisher was close at hand, and Vik put the flames out in a matter of seconds, but this was too much.

"There's evil in this house," Sam said quietly.

"I didn't know you believed in that sort of thing," Anu responded.

"I didn't, but I do now. You two have to get out of here. Whatever it is that possesses this old place hates you, and it won't stop tormenting you until you're gone—one way or another. Don't risk pushing this evil force to its limit. It won't end well."

That afternoon, Anu and Vik locked up the house that they'd hoped would be their dream home and never went back. All the cleaning and renovating they'd done helped to sell it quickly. They hesitated about whether or not to tell the buyers of their own terrifying encounters, but when they saw the bright smiles of anticipation on the other young couple's faces, they decided to be honest. Unfortunately for that hopeful pair, they only looked at one another and rolled their eyes. A month later, they too moved out.

When the house went back up for sale, the townsfolk banded together and bought it for a community hall. Exactly two weeks later, the building, thankfully empty at the time, burned to the ground. Despite an intensive investigation, the official cause of the fire was recorded as "unknown."

Today, a stylish new summer home stands on that beautiful spot near both the road and the lake. A happy family holidays there every summer, blissfully unaware of the bizarre history associated with the location.

BRICHT AS NICHT

Nikhil scrunched the paper-thin motel pillow—again—and checked the clock on the bedside table—again. The luminous green numbers shone 2:06, four minutes later than the last time he'd looked. People had warned him that it was tough to get any sleep in Inuvik during summer because the sun simply never set. He'd slept well enough the first three nights, but apparently his luck wasn't going to hold for this final night in this small Northwest Territories town.

Exasperation forced him out of bed. He pulled on the jeans and shirt that he'd tossed on the chair some hours before and stepped outside. What a sight: broad daylight in the middle of the night! The sunshine was warm and the fresh air felt good. He crossed the parking lot to the sidewalk. Main Street could have been a ghost town: the stores had been closed for hours, but the sun glinted off every window, door, and sign.

Nikhil kicked at a pebble and sent it flying half a block. It landed next to a vending machine beside a drugstore. Maybe a snack would help settle him down. He shoved two loonies into the coin slot and chose a box of chocolate-coated raisins. The machine stayed silent and still. He slammed his hand against the glass. Nothing. He shoved his shoulder against the metal side panel. Nothing. Now he really wanted those raisins. He fished in his pocket for two more loonies. Still no joy. He could walk away, but then the vending machine would have beaten him, just like the constant daylight had. He hammered at the machine with the side of his fist and heard something rattle inside. He hammered a second time and, like manna from heaven, a box of chocolate-coated raisins dropped into the tray below.

He grabbed his hard-won prize from the machine. *Four-dollar raisins. Probably stale, too,* he thought. He poured half a dozen raisins into his hand before putting the package into his shirt pocket. To his surprise, they were fresh and tasty. Better still, his mood lifted as the sugar hit his system.

Other than tonight's insomnia, he'd enjoyed his stay in Inuvik. Usually he didn't fare too well away from home, but this trip had been different. He'd never seen the North before, and its grandeur had left him awestruck. He walked on, reasoning that if he wasn't going to be able to sleep, then he might as well get one more look at the mighty Mackenzie River.

A man sat on a park bench near the river. No doubt another out-of-towner unable to sleep. Nik approached the stranger and nodded. The man returned the gesture and moved over on the bench as if to invite Nikhil to join him. *Perhaps we could help each other pass the long, bright night,* thought Nik.

Nik sat down and took the box of raisins out of his pocket. "Care for a bit of candy from a dishonest vending machine?"

"Thanks," the man said quietly, shaking some raisins into his hand.

"Got sent up here from Lethbridge. My boss wanted a site checked out before he bid on a project. Been here since Monday, but I fly out late tomorrow—I guess, technically, today now," Nikhil said, looking over at the man.

The stranger must have been a handsome man in his day, but time had taken its toll. His eyes were red-rimmed and sunk deep in their sockets—a sure sign of insomnia.

"Do you have a souvenir of your time in Inuvik?" the stranger asked.

Nik chuckled. "I'm not much of a souvenir collector, actually."

"I have something you might like."

The man reached into his jacket pocket and Nikhil tensed. *A gun?*

No, just a piece of paper—a very old piece of paper, judging from the looks of it. The man's hands shook as he held the sheet toward Nikhil. A stylized drawing of a bear took up most of the piece of paper, but someone had also made detailed notes around the margins.

"Let me tell you the story behind this," said the stranger. "It's only a copy, but it's still worth something. It took me weeks—and that's why I might as well give it away."

Intrigued, Nikhil listened as the man continued. "I'm a forger. Counterfeiting's been my career and it's served me well, but you can see for yourself that my hands aren't steady anymore. It's the kiss of death in this trade. If a forger's going to be of any use to anyone, he has to be quick and he has to be steady. I'm neither now. What I am, frankly, is worried. There aren't exactly good pension plans in my line of work."

Nikhil was taken aback by the man's candour. Their odd circumstances, sleepless strangers in the middle of a bright, sunshiny night seemed to have created a strange intimacy. The two sat in silence for a moment. Nik looked more closely at the drawing. It would look terrific framed and hanging on his living room wall. He'd have a real conversation starter. Yes, actually, he would like the drawing, he told the old man. "What's it a copy of?" he asked.

"You've heard of the Indigenous carver Nathaniel Benjamin? He lived most of his life in a cabin west of here. He died years ago now, so his work goes up in value every year as more people get to see and appreciate his artistry with soapstone. He always did a detailed sketch before he started a carving. Then, as soon as the sculpture was complete, he'd burn the sketch."

"I remember reading about that," said Nik. "He died before he could complete his last work. It was the most ambitious project he'd ever taken on."

The man nodded. "It was this bear. A museum owns the unfinished sculpture. The original drawing's there, too. Copying from the masters like Benjamin, that's how I honed my craft and supported myself. These last two weeks, the people at the museum must've wondered about me—sitting there for hours, staring at a piece of paper, but it was something I needed to do. I had to find out if I still had it in me. I don't. I knew this day would come."

"I'd like to give you something for your work," Nikhil told the man.

"Wouldn't take anything for it. I'm starting fresh. Please, let this be my first honest transaction."

"Will you be all right?"

The man didn't acknowledge the question. He stood up, nodded, and said, "Best of luck to you."

"You too," Nikhil called out, but the man had already walked away. Strangely, the angle of the sun's rays made it seem as though he had simply vanished.

Nik walked back to his motel room, lay the fragile drawing on the night table, and stretched out on the bed, telling himself that he would fall asleep. But he knew better. The forger's story churned in his mind. He picked up the small drawing; the paper was fragile. So strange to think that it had just been made this week—stranger even than the twenty-four-hour daylight.

Discomfort surged through Nikhil's body. He pulled the thin blanket around himself and curled into a fetal position. *This is ridiculous. I've been reduced to a shivering child.* He went into the bathroom and splashed cold water on his face; that always made him feel better. But when he looked up into the old cracked mirror, he gasped. Years had been added to his face in less than an hour. He was pale. His eyes were red-rimmed and sunk back in their sockets.

Nikhil swung around toward the door. Someone was watching him, he was sure. But that was ridiculous—there couldn't be anyone watching him, because there was no one else in the room.

A waft of cool air brushed past Nikhil's back, as though someone had just walked behind him—but no one could have: he was leaning against the bathroom wall. Heavy footsteps plodded across the floor above him—except that there wasn't a floor above him. The motel was only one storey high. Nikhil jammed his fist into his mouth to keep from screaming.

"Give my drawing back," an angry voice hissed.

Nikhil lunged for the door, pausing only to pick up the drawing. He had to find the man who had given him the cursed thing. There'd be no conversation starter hanging on his living room wall—that much he knew.

He bolted from the motel and ran back to the river front. If the man was there, he could give the drawing back to him. But the man was nowhere to be seen. It didn't matter. Nik was getting rid of the paper. He grabbed the raisin box from his shirt pocket. In a panic, he shook the last three candies from the package onto the ground and stuffed the drawing into the empty box. He pulled the last three loonies from his change pocket and jammed them into the box for weight. Then he threw the box into the swiftly flowing Mackenzie River.

There, it was gone. Whatever it was.

With an unsteady gait, Nikhil shuffled back to his motel room.

By five o'clock that morning, he had fallen into a fitful sleep. An hour later, the alarm clock rang. He felt worse than he could ever remember feeling. He needed to get home—soon, very soon, as soon as he possibly could.

The desperation he felt must have been evident in his voice, because the reservation clerk who took his phone call about the possibility of an earlier flight didn't question Nikhil's request or mention anything about additional fees. She switched his booking from the evening flight to the first one out in the afternoon, and Nikhil was at the airport well ahead of the time she'd specified. He went into the washroom but averted his eyes to avoid looking in the mirror. He never wanted to see that haunted look again.

He fished his phone out of his carry-on bag and tried to get into some Fortnite, but found he couldn't concentrate. Time would drag if he didn't have something to distract him, so he picked up a freebie copy of the local newspaper.

There, on the front page, was a photograph of the drawing Nikhil had thrown into the river. The man's story had been a lie. The drawing he had given Nikhil wasn't a copy: it was the original, stolen from the museum the day before. Police presumed that the thief had been trying to get the priceless, unfinished last work of Nathaniel Benjamin, but a security guard had interrupted him and the man had fled, dropping a poorly made copy of Benjamin's sketch near the sculpture. The original drawing was missing.

A weight crushed in on Nikhil's chest. He lurched back to the airport washroom, pushed open a stall door, and leaned against it while violent shakes ricocheted through his body.

If only he didn't understand the consequences of what he'd done. But he did. He'd destroyed an invaluable artefact and angered the spirit that possessed it. How much damage—and to whom—had he caused?

When his flight was called, Nikhil made his way toward the gate, his legs so unsteady that moving them required a conscious effort. All he could think was that in mere moments, he would be flying away from the entire experience. Unfortunately, he didn't believe his thought—nor would he ever again truly believe anything.

SAVIOUR AT SEA

Lawrence and Maurice were brothers who lived on the northeast shore of New Brunswick. Like most of the men who lived in the area, they were fishermen. They had a boat that others envied, the *Edna*. She was a sturdy three-master, and they kept her shipshape.

Despite those advantages, there were still times when fishing wasn't an easy way to make a living. Sometimes they had to sail a good way out into the Atlantic to catch enough to make the trip worth their while. And so it was on one day when the wind had died down, leaving them becalmed on a sea as flat as a mill pond. There was nothing either Lawrence or Maurice could do except wait it out, but even by sundown there wasn't so much as a hint of a breeze.

When the sun had set and darkness had settled around them, the brothers began to worry.

"I can smell a storm brewing," Lawrence said, and Maurice nodded. They both knew they could be in for serious trouble.

When they felt the first zephyr flutter through the sails, they didn't know whether to feel grateful or more afraid. They'd barely had time to make up their minds when a gale blew up, bringing harsh winds and rain. There was no time to waver now: they needed to find a port. Within minutes, the roar of the wind was deafening, whipping their voices away no matter how loudly they yelled to one another.

The *Edna* slammed into the crests of the waves and crashed down into the valleys over and over again. Seawater sluiced across the deck while the two men hung on for dear life, one at the wheel, one on the rigging. Rain pounded at them like needles on their exposed faces.

Hours passed. The brothers were exhausted. They resigned themselves to the inevitable. They knew the sea would win. It always did.

Then, from a distance, Maurice spotted a faint light. Could it be a lighthouse? Were they close to land? But no, this light was moving, lurching along at an uneven gait over the waves. Maurice rubbed his eyes and looked again. He hadn't been imagining the glowing white ball bouncing oddly toward them. He called to Lawrence and pointed toward the strange circle of light. Lawrence nodded. *So he can see it, too,* Maurice thought. *Surely we can't be sharing the same delusion . . .*

As the shining orb grew closer, they could see that it was a lantern. Beside it was a glowing figure. Soon, the lights were close enough to the *Edna* that both Maurice and Lawrence could make out the shape of a human being: a very old woman leaning on a cane with one hand and holding a lantern in the other.

Death, they each thought to themselves. *This must be death coming for us.* They cowered down on their boat deck in terror.

Many hours passed. The brothers drifted in and out of consciousness. Every time they opened their eyes, they could see the luminescent figure with the lantern still floating nearby. Stranger still, they could feel their boat moving as though it were being sailed by an expert mariner.

Then both the light and the figure were gone. The sudden darkness roused the two exhausted men to their feet. As they stood, they saw another light off on the horizon. It was a lighthouse, and not just any lighthouse: it was the one nearest their home. That hadn't been death that had come to them. It had been their saviour—although they had no idea who she might have been. They offered prayers of gratitude to their unknown rescuer.

Less than an hour later, they were home safely, sitting at the kitchen table while their mother served them bowls of hot soup. She was so relieved to see them that, at first, she didn't even want to hear the harrowing details of how they lived through the storm. The next morning, though, they told her about the figure with the cane and the lantern. As Lawrence described the presence, their mother clung to the arm of her chair, the colour draining from her face.

"Wait right there," she told her sons.

A moment later, she returned with a very old photograph. It was a picture of an elderly woman leaning on a cane. The brothers looked at the photo closely. It was faded, but they could make out the woman's features well enough to recognize her.

"This was my grandmother," their mother said. "She was dead before either of you were born."

Maurice and Lawrence stared at their mother. She drew in a deep breath and said, "In life, she was like a second mother to me, and now, in death, she saved my sons for me."

Neither Maurice nor Lawrence said a word. There was nothing to say. They knew their mother was right. Their long-dead great-grandmother had rescued them from a lethal storm in the North Atlantic.

GRANDPA'S FAVOURITE STORY

The Roaring Twenties was a time like no other in Canada's history. The Great War had finally ended, leaving in its wake not only a booming economy but also an entire generation of citizens ready to appreciate the economic upsurge and enjoy life more fully than ever before. And no two people were better prepared to take advantage of the newly created atmosphere of freedom than Willard and Amelia. They were young, they were ambitious, and they were engaged to be married. They were certain that their prosperity and happiness were assured. To that end, the couple moved to Toronto from the small lakeside community where they had been raised.

Toronto in the late 1920s was an exciting place to be. During the day, Willard worked at an insurance agency. He was intelligent and, perhaps more important, he was industrious. Although he was hired only to do clerical work, he welcomed every opportunity to show that he could do more.

Before long, Willard's hard work was rewarded; he was made a junior partner in the firm. On the afternoon of his promotion, Willard could hardly wait to see his beloved Amelia to share the good news with her. She could finally quit her job as a typist and the two could marry and start the family they both wanted.

The clock above Willard's desk seemed to take at least twice as long as usual to get to 5:00 PM. At quitting time, he all but flew from the office. Even though the firm's senior partners were used to their young "apprentice" staying behind until all his work was finished, they were not upset. Quite to the contrary, they were delighted, because they knew that he was rushing off to plan the rest of his life—a life that would include extraordinary loyalty to their firm.

By the time he arrived outside the building where Amelia worked, Willard was out of breath. He was also early. She would not be free to leave work for another few minutes. He took the time to compose himself, catch his breath, and enjoy the anticipation of the moment. That enjoyment became so all-encompassing that when Amelia did make her way to his side, he was completely lost in thought.

For her part, Amelia was so pleased to see Willard that she did not notice the faraway look in his eyes. She certainly didn't expect that her simple, enthusiastic greeting of "Hello" would startle him, but it succeeded in doing exactly that. His jumpy response told Amelia that her normally relaxed loved one was bursting with excitement. She could hardly wait to hear his news.

Arm in arm, the young couple strolled through the Toronto streets, planning the most wonderful future possible.

"And children, Willard, we must have children," Amelia declared as they strolled through the grounds of Queen's Park.

"We will have the finest children in the world," Willard confirmed without hesitation.

Neither direction nor distance had meant anything to the couple as they'd walked and talked, but now, as they approached a park bench, they decided to rest for a while. Their chatter about the future continued, but as Willard was extolling the sterling qualities that their future children would possess, Amelia slowly became more and more distracted. She thought she could hear the sounds of a baby crying somewhere very close at hand.

It's just my imagination, she thought. *It's because we're talking about babies—that's why I think I'm hearing those cries.*

Finally, the piteous wails completely diverted Amelia's concentration and she interrupted Willard to ask if he heard them, too. The still-excited man stopped talking mid-sentence and turned his head at an angle.

"Yes, you're right. There is a baby crying nearby," he confirmed.

The couple hurried toward the plaintive sounds. But no matter how far they walked, they always seemed to be the same distance away from the disturbing noise. The sun was setting, and the growing darkness led the pair to assume that they were merely having trouble seeing the child among the shadows. Their own joy set aside temporarily, Willard and Amelia concentrated on finding the source of the cries. They could certainly not leave while an infant lay abandoned in the park!

Their search had thus far been fruitless and frustrating. When Willard and Amelia happened upon a policeman strolling through the park, they were relieved at the prospect of having someone in authority to help them in their mission. They hurried toward the uniformed officer.

In their mounting concern for the unseen baby's well-being, the two spoke simultaneously and far too quickly to be understood. Even so, the policeman was calm. He knew exactly what it was that had this young couple so upset. They were merely the latest in a long line of people to hear the phantom cries of a deceased child—cries that were so poignant and real that he knew it would take quite a lot of convincing to call off the search party that these two were probably already envisioning.

Fortunately, he had done this before. With as much patience as he could muster, the kindly Toronto policeman explained, "Those cries that you heard were from another dimension. That child is no longer in this time or place—only his cries are left with us."

Even though it was twilight, the officer could tell by the expressions on their faces that the young couple was shocked by his words. He also knew that this was not the last time he would have to give this same explanation to concerned citizens. People had been hearing the little soul's cries for years, and he expected that they would for many years to come.

When they were convinced that the policeman knew what he was talking about, Willard and Amelia left the park and headed to a downtown restaurant for dinner. The excited chatter that had marked their trip to the park had been replaced by silence. Although they felt they had little choice but to accept the policeman's words as truth, neither of them could quite believe what they had just heard—neither the pitiful wailing nor the officer's chilling explanation of the sound.

Months, even years, later—long after they'd married and started their family—Willard and Amelia would often discuss that memorable evening in Queen's Park, wondering about the tiny infant responsible for the mournful crying that they and so many others had heard.

The autumn of 1929 did not bring much that was positive to the world. It did, however, mark the end of something negative. After that time, the phantom cries of the ghostly infant in Queen's Park were no longer heard. At last, the spirit had gone on to their eternal rest.

Thanks to one couple's compassion, neither the tiny tormented soul nor its plight were ever forgotten. As soon as their own children were old enough to hear the story, Willard and Amelia told and retold their strange experience to their two sons. When those two boys grew into men and later married and had children of their own, they shared the "true" ghost story with their own kids. The tale became known as "Grandpa's Favourite Story."

And so, because of this family's intergenerational storytelling, the suffering child was finally given the attention they had cried out for—even though it was long after their death.

ISLAND ENTITIES

Prince Edward Island may not have a large population of flesh-and-blood citizens, but it certainly has a good-sized collection of ghostly legends! This poignant tale concerns a haunted house in Abrams Village, on the west coast of the Island.

At one time, the story goes, a cruel woman and her disabled husband lived there. All their neighbours knew she was nasty to her poor husband, and they tried to help out when they could, but at certain times, in the evenings for instance, those good folks were in their own homes with their own families. And that was when the wife usually tormented the helpless man. One of the tricks she liked to play on him was to bring his dinner to a table near his chair—but she put his plate just far enough away that he couldn't reach it. This went on for so long that it is said her cruelty and its effects embedded themselves in the very atmosphere of the house where they lived.

By the time a young couple named Bill and Kate owned the house in the 1980s, that first couple had been dead for many years. Clearly, though, their essences had remained.

One evening, as Bill sat in the living room relaxing, Kate was in the kitchen making a pot of coffee for the two of them. When the brew was ready, she carried two steaming mugs out into the living room, setting one down on a small table near her husband. Bill thanked his wife for the drink, took a sip, and set the mug back down on the table.

Soon, he reached for his cup again—but the cup wasn't where he had put it down only a moment before. Now it was on the far side of the table.

Thinking that Kate was playing a silly prank, he simply reached for the mug, drank from it, and put it back beside him on the table. Moments later, the scene replayed itself.

Wondering what he was up against—a wife in a playful mood or something more puzzling—Bill turned his full attention to the coffee cup. Seconds later, he watched in amazement as his cup moved away from him. His wife certainly was not involved: she had not moved from her chair across the room. Only the cup had moved, and once again he had to reach for it.

Bill began to wonder if there was something supernatural at work in their house, so he decided to make discreet inquiries around town and listened carefully to stories that the old folks in the community told. Soon he understood why his coffee cup had moved seemingly of its own volition. Their house, like many on Prince Edward Island, was haunted.

He never told Kate about his suspicions, though, because he knew she'd be terrified. He solved the problem by suggesting that they drink their after-dinner coffee at the kitchen table.

—

Another story from Prince Edward Island is as heart-warming as the previous one was heart-wrenching.

A miller lived in Queens County, in the southwest of the Island. He was well liked within the community because he was honest and friendly, and turned out high-quality flour. The story begins when he and his family became ill and were confined to their beds. The mill, their only source of income, stood still and silent in the yard adjacent to their home. There was grain to be milled, but the miller was too ill to attend to it.

One night, the miller and his family were awakened by the sound of the machinery working in the mill next door. Thinking that intruders had broken in, the man gathered all his strength about him and, arming himself with as large a stick as he could find, headed out to investigate.

He pulled open the door to the mill. Inside, all the presses were working smoothly, yet the place was completely dark. He could hear footsteps echoing over the noise of the running equipment, but he couldn't see anyone inside. Moments later, when his eyes had adjusted to his dark surroundings, he saw the shape of a man. Too surprised to speak or even move, the miller watched this mysterious image as it went about operating the mill in a way so familiar to its owner.

When he was able to collect his wits, the miller called to the presence. The sound of his own voice put a sudden end to all the activity. Even more puzzled now, he lit as many lanterns as he was able to find from his spot near the door into the building. He could see no one. No one passed him to leave the mill and yet, there, not far from where he stood, were three bags of milled grain.

A phantom had come during the night to help the sick and near-destitute family.

STORIES BY MOONLIGHT

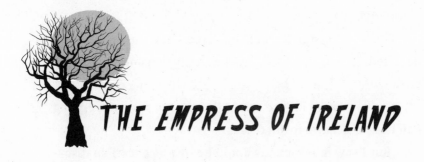

THE EMPRESS OF IRELAND

This story begins on a tiny, remote island named Fair Isle, off the northern coast of Scotland. The date was May 29, 1914. It was a Sunday morning, and most of the seventy-two islanders were in church. The postmaster, Jerome Stout, was one of the most respected men on the island and especially well known for paying rapt attention to the minister's weekly sermon. But this Sunday was different. This Sunday, Jerome Stout spent the entire service staring intently out the church window. One of the fishermen from the village couldn't help but notice this breach of etiquette, and after the final benediction was pronounced and the congregation made its way out into the fresh air, the man approached Stout.

"I'd say you owe the minister an apology," the fisherman said. "You were looking out the window the whole while you were in church."

Stout shook his head. For a moment, he looked dazed and unaware of his surroundings. Slowly, his mind seemed to ease back into his body.

"I'm sorry," Stout said. "I tried to look away, but I couldn't."

"But there was nothing out there to be seen," the fisherman countered.

The postmaster rubbed his eyes. "But there *was*," he declared. "It was dreadful. I was watching an enormous ship go down."

The fisherman looked out at the choppy sea surrounding Fair Isle. "I see no ship out there."

"But I saw it as clear as could be. It was a terrible disaster. There were two ships, and they were both fogbound. The small ship rammed an enormous ocean liner, hit her midship in a dense fog. It was pandemonium. Hundreds and hundreds of people were screaming for their lives and throwing themselves into the icy-cold waves. There was an unimaginable loss of life; so many were carried under the waves to their watery graves."

The fisherman was taken aback. He didn't know what to make of the story that Stout had just told him. After all, the man was usually as sober as a judge and definitely not given to telling tall tales. Both men shook their heads as they walked away from each other, thinking that they would never speak of the strange matter again.

But several days later, when the mail boat arrived at Fair Isle, the islanders were astonished to read of a maritime collision in the St. Lawrence River near Rimouski in Quebec. In the wee hours of May 29, the air above the river was so thick with fog that there was virtually no visibility. The *Storstad*, a small Norwegian coal ship, had struck the *Empress of Ireland*, an enormous ocean liner that was outbound at full speed from Quebec City to Liverpool.

The larger ship sank to the bottom of the river within fourteen minutes of the strike. Hundreds and hundreds of people from the *Empress* jumped for their lives into the frigid water that became their grave. Of the 1,477 aboard, 1,012 drowned. To this day, the *Empress of Ireland* tragedy remains the worst Canadian maritime disaster during peacetime.

And somehow, postmaster Jerome Stout witnessed the horrors of the fatal collision thousands of kilometres away on the tiny, remote island of Fair Isle in Scotland.

THE TRAIN WRECK

All winter, Andrew and Jessica and their sons, Nicholas and Aidan, looked forward to their annual summer camping trip to their favourite campground. They always left their home in Moosomin, Saskatchewan, the day the boys finished school for the year. Usually, as soon as they had shown their parents their report cards, both boys helped pack the family's trailer and soon they were all ready and eager to get on the road. This particular summer, though, Jessica was delayed at work and the family wasn't able to get away until well into the evening. They considered postponing and not leaving until the next morning, but decided to push through and keep their tradition alive. And so it was that they were heading west at ten o'clock that night.

Soon, Nicholas and Aidan were both asleep in the back seat.

"We need to stop for gas before we hit the highway," Andrew said.

Jessica nodded sleepily. She had had a long day at work and was dead tired. She rolled up her sweater to use as a pillow and pushed it against the car window. A moment later, she, too, was fast asleep.

At the station, Andrew got out of the car and chatted with the station attendant as the man pumped the gas.

"Looks like the pressure on your trailer's right front tire's a bit low," the attendant commented. "Our air pump's not working at the moment, otherwise I'd top it up for you. Sorry about that."

Andrew thanked the man for noticing and told him he'd see to it in the morning. The family was soon back on the road, with everyone—except Andrew, of course—dreaming happy dreams of their campsite.

The kilometres went by on the dark, deserted highway until suddenly Andrew felt the steering wheel pull hard to the right. *It must be that tire on the trailer,* he realized as he struggled to maintain control of the car and get them safely to the side of the road. The sudden change in movement woke Jessica, and she watched silently as her husband fought to get the car and trailer safely to the side of the road. Nicholas and Aidan slept peacefully through the incident.

"Whew," said Andrew as he let out the breath he'd been holding as he manoeuvred the vehicle to a stop.

"Well done," Jessica said, giving his shoulder a squeeze.

"Wait here. I'll go out and try to see exactly what happened."

A moment later he was back in the car. "That tire blew, the one the guy said was low on pressure. We can't drive any farther till it's fixed."

"What are we going to do?" Jessica asked, trying to hide her concern.

"I'll have to go get help, I guess. You wait here with the boys and all the gear."

Jessica was not the least bit pleased at the thought of her husband walking or hitchhiking along the darkened highway, but she also knew there was no alternative. She peered through the windshield, trying to watch Andrew as he walked away, but the night shadows swallowed him up in no time.

Maybe I can fall sleep again, she thought but soon realized she was far too tense, so she just stared out into the inky darkness, wishing desperately that they'd postponed their departure until morning.

After a while, despite her jangled nerves, Jessica fell into a fitful sleep, dreaming the awful dreams you have when you're stressed and exhausted. Then the piercing sound of a train whistle jolted her out of unconsciousness. She sat up and gazed apprehensively into the dark night. There was nothing. She turned around to check on the kids. They were fine. Jessica rearranged the sweater, her temporary pillow, and closed her eyes again, this time to say a prayer for poor Andrew alone out there in the night.

When she opened her eyes again, Jessica thought she could see a small light off in the distance. *Maybe that's Andrew coming back*, she thought, relief flooding through her. She sat up straighter and looked out again. The light was coming closer. A moment later, her heart sank. The light was huge, far too large to be the beam of a flashlight. It was a train's headlight. Funny, she didn't remember railroad tracks near here. The light came closer still until she could see the locomotive. It was an old-fashioned one—a steam engine—and it was travelling along an old wooden trestle bridge.

Jessica blinked several times and strained to see if her eyes were playing tricks on her. This couldn't be. There couldn't possibly be a steam train puffing along nonexistent tracks on a nonexistent bridge.

But the longer Jessica looked, the more clearly she saw a train chugging across her field of vision, a good twenty metres higher than the road. *It must be a passenger train*, she thought. She could clearly see people sitting in the brightly lit coaches.

Then, in an instant, the train cars jackknifed. A terrible grinding sound ripped through the air. *How can Aidan and Nicholas be sleeping through this?* she wondered as one by one, the cars—first the steam engine, then the tender car, then the coaches, and finally, the caboose—fell from the bridge and crashed into the valley below.

Jessica jumped out of the car. She could hear the screams from those on board as they dropped to certain death. She ran to the edge of the valley and looked down at the utter carnage. Bodies lay strewn in a field of metal debris. Most of the coaches lay on their sides, their wheels still turning. Other than that, nothing moved and all was silent. Jessica covered her face with her hands and sobbed with sadness and frustration.

A moment later she heard a voice, a man's voice. "Andrew?" she called out, but there was no answer. She turned, and there, standing beside her, was a stranger, a man dressed in black-and-white-striped overalls and wearing a black-and-white-striped cap. He held a large pocket watch out toward her and said, "Hello." Jessica's mouth opened and she tried to reply, but no sound came out. Then the man asked, "Can you tell me the time, please?"

She looked at her watch and answered him in a whisper, the only sound she could make at that moment. "It's 11:20 PM, but what does that matter right now? There's been such a horrible accident! All those poor people must be dead."

Then it occurred to Jessica that perhaps this man was dangerous. She started to back away from him, watching him all the while. By the time she was three metres or so away from him, the man no longer seemed to be solid, but rather his body seemed to be made up of tiny dots of light. She looked again. Now he was little more than a cloud of mist. Finally, he had disappeared entirely.

"Jessica!" She heard a welcome, familiar voice call her name. It was Andrew. He was walking toward her with a young man at his side.

"Andrew, I'm so glad to see you. Look, down there in the valley. A passenger train crashed from the trestle. I watched the whole thing. It was awful," she said, nearly hysterical.

The two men shone oversized flashlights down into the valley.

"There's no train down there, Jess," her husband said, thinking that this would reassure his wife.

"There is!" she exclaimed. "I saw it fall from the bridge. There were dozens of people on board. We have to help them."

"Jessie, I think you must have been dreaming. I don't think the train even runs along here anymore." Gently, Andrew led his wife back to the car, where their sons slept peacefully.

Andrew and the young man who'd offered to come with him to help replace the trailer tire had the rig up on a hoist in no time. Once they had replaced the tire, they drove to the closest town and dropped their helper off at the twenty-four–hour service station where he worked. There was a motel near the station, so they decided they'd stay there for the rest of the night.

"Let's just forget about everything that's happened tonight. We'll start out again fresh tomorrow, and that will be the first day of our holiday," Andrew suggested.

"We're not starting out for anywhere until I've checked out that train crash I saw," Jessica said emphatically.

And so it was that the next morning, they drove into town and found the local train station. Jessica went in and explained the horrible train wreck she had witnessed the night before. An elderly man behind the counter listened patiently as she described watching the steam locomotive and the passenger cars topple from the bridge into the valley below.

The man nodded and then paused before he spoke. "I don't exactly know how to tell you this, ma'am, but that accident you saw didn't happen last night."

"It did. I was there. I saw it happen," Jessica implored.

"I don't doubt that you saw it," the man said, "but it didn't happen last night. That accident happened well over a hundred years ago. You're not the first to report seeing it."

Jessica stood speechless.

"I have an old newspaper report about the crash. Let me get it for you," the man said as he went to a filing cabinet. He flipped through an armful of file folders. "Here it is. I haven't looked at this for ages."

He held an old, yellowed clipping up so both he and Jessica could see it.

"Well, would you look at that," he said. "What a coincidence. See the date at the top? That accident happened on yesterday's date, June 28, but over a hundred years ago."

Jessica mumbled her thanks and slowly walked from the train office into the bright sunshine, where her husband and sons waited impatiently for her. As she walked, scenes from the dreadful accident she had witnessed played in her head: the steam engine, the brightly lit passenger coaches with people silhouetted on the windows. The scream of the twisted metal and then the terrible silence. A shudder ran through her body. She didn't know what had happened to her last night at the side of the road, but one thing she did know for certain. "No more camping trips for me," she said to Andrew. "Next year we're going on a cruise instead!"

SOUL SOLD CHEAP

Far up on the rugged northern shore of Labrador, there once stood an abandoned house. There had always been rumours that the place was haunted, but only a few remaining old-timers knew that those stories weren't just rumours. It seemed that decades ago, a very greedy man named Tobias had lived in that house. He had more money than anyone he knew, but even so, Tobias wanted more.

Tobias was alone in his house on a particularly stormy night when the icy winds off the North Atlantic Ocean blew so hard that the windows of his house rattled threateningly. He had no neighbours and certainly no friends to call on, so instead he called to Lucifer, the Devil himself.

Moments later, flames shot down the chimney and there, standing in front of Tobias, was the fallen angel. In no time, the two wretches had come to an agreement. They decided that every night, the greedy man would hang his boots by the chimney and the Devil would fill those boots with gold.

In return, all the Devil wanted was Tobias's soul.

But not until the man had died, you understand.

Once that deal was struck, Tobias was as happy as a greedy, lonely man could possibly be. Surprisingly, Lucifer kept his word, and each morning the man collected his gold and gleefully stacked it on his table. Then he took a moment to tell himself what a clever negotiator he was.

One night, it occurred to Tobias that if this much gold made him happy, then even more gold would make him even happier. He thought and thought until he came up with a plan, one that he thought was devilishly clever, if he did say so himself. He cut the soles out of his boots. This way, when the Devil poured the gold into them, it would all run through and fill not just his boots but the entire room.

Sure enough, his dastardly plan worked, and early the next morning Tobias happily waded in to a room that was knee-deep in gold.

Of course, Lucifer was no one's fool—certainly not Tobias's fool, anyway—so the Devil simply stopped coming around to deliver the gold every night. Eventually, the greedy man died, and when he did, he felt safe in his assumption that Lucifer had broken their contract. Sadly, he was mistaken. Apparently the Devil never forgives his part of any bargain, and so the minute Tobias's heart stopped beating, the Devil claimed his soul. Worse, Lucifer even felt quite self-righteous about his evil deed because the man had tried to fool him.

Tobias was buried in a plot near his home. His gravestone was a simple one, bearing only five words: *Tobias lived and died here.* It was many years before someone looked at the engraving on that stone closely enough to realize that the word "lived" was the word "devil" spelled backward. It made sense, because by that time, everyone in the area knew the miserable old man's house on the rugged cliff was well and truly haunted.

Many families who were down on their luck tried living in the house, but none lasted more than a few nights. They all reported hearing footfalls echoing from empty rooms and watching in fright as lights went on and off when no one was near them. The worst, though, they all agreed, was the dreadful draft that swept down the chimney and sent an unnatural chill into the air.

The place stood abandoned for many years until finally, the local shoemaker, a man who didn't believe in such nonsense as hauntings, began operating his business from the house. But even he didn't last too long. You see, every evening when he hung the boots he'd made on pegs by the chimney, those boots would fly across the room, as if an invisible hand had thrown them.

GUARDIAN OF THE LAKE

On Cape Breton Island in Nova Scotia, there is a lake, it is said, that is watched over by a supernatural being. This lake is dark, silent, and still—and more than a little menacing. Some say the lake's unnatural being is a guardian, perhaps an ancient grandfather. Others say the presence is a demon. All that is known for certain is that the spirit of the lake does not like to be disturbed. The only flesh-and-blood beings that have ever dared to disrespect the lake's supernatural power are the occasional teenaged boys—those who are far too cool (or foolish) to be frightened away by tall tales.

Noah and Jeremy were two such foolish boys. Somehow, they had managed to convince their friend Mac to come along with them on their camping expedition to the haunted lake. But Mac was such a wimp: just as they knew he would, on the first night, their friend was hiding in the tent, reading by flashlight. Actually, they weren't even sure he was reading: they just knew that he had the flashlight right beside him, turned on to its brightest setting.

As it turned out, the foolhardy boys were right in their guess that Mac wasn't reading. He was huddled in his sleeping bag, flashlight in hand, silently calling out to his long-dead father, who, years ago, had told him the legend about the guardian of the lake.

"The being is ugly," his father had told him, before adding that its hair smelled like rotting weeds and its skin was covered in scales.

After a while, Mac opened the tent flap and looked out to see what the other boys were doing. As he did, a dark shape formed over the lake. Meanwhile, Noah and Jeremy were throwing rocks as far out into the lake as they could hurl them, oblivious to the ominous-looking shape.

The shape thickened until Mac could see its dead, red eyes. Moments later, something grabbed Mac's friends by the legs and dragged them out into the lake. The boys kicked and screamed and fought to get free, but the thing had each of them in a solid hold. Soon, those boys were at the bottom of the lake.

Calmly, Mac watched the bubbles from his friends' last gasps of air rise to the surface of the water.

Then the bubbles stopped. Slowly, Mac morphed back into a teenaged boy in a tent pitched beside the lake—the lake that his spirit haunted—the lake that was his grave—the lake that no one would ever disrespect.

VILLAGE VISITOR

Once upon a time, there was a tiny community in northern Alberta. How tiny was it, you ask? The place was so small that from September to June, it didn't exist at all. You see, the cluster of cabins that comprised it was officially classified as a "summer village." Despite its temporary status, the same campers came back year after year, and over time, they established many happy traditions.

One of the most popular of those traditions was Skit Night, an evening when all the campers gathered in the nearby field and entertained one another. People would plan and rehearse their presentations weeks in advance. Some of those performances became the stuff of legends. A few years ago, for instance, Ernie's contribution had everyone laughing when he appeared on "stage" (really just some plywood sheets laid on the ground) wearing his pajamas and standing beside a stack of old car tires. Finally, he had had to tell the audience that this was his way of announcing that he was going to "retire." Then you could always count on Fred and his youngest son playing their guitars—badly. And each year's crop of kids would put on a play that made absolutely no sense to anyone, but the audience applauded just the same. The routine might sound like it was corny, but the campers loved it just that way.

One summer, a young woman driving an old camper van arrived just as the fun was getting underway. The stranger parked, got out, and leaned against her van as she watched the campers move mismatched lawn chairs into place and shuffle props around.

Word soon spread about the visiting van and its occupant, so, not wanting to seem rude, some of the campers waved to the woman, inviting her to join them. They were tickled when she took a violin case out of the van and slowly made her way toward the crowd.

"The more the merrier," an elderly man called out to the new arrival. "Especially on such a gorgeous summer's night," he added, gesturing toward the clear sky and bright, full moon.

The woman nodded in response to the invitation and moved to the back of the gathering, where she had a straight sightline to all the goings-on, but none of the campers could see her without craning their necks—which no one did, of course, because it wouldn't have been polite.

And although the campers didn't know it at the time, this arrangement was just the way the stranger wanted it to be. She wasn't interested in any of them—well, that wasn't quite true. She was only interested in one of them, a young man wearing a dark-blue tank top. She could see that his shoulders were heavily muscled and even his neck was thick with ropey muscles. His arms were fully decorated with tattoos.

His neck would look good marked, too, she thought as she stared at him.

By the time all of the planned performances were over, the sun had started to set, but then someone remembered their visitor with the violin and encouraged her to take the stage. At first she seemed reluctant, but then she smiled shyly at the audience's welcoming applause and walked to the front of the group, all the while keeping her eye on the tattooed man in the blue tank top.

She took her violin and bow out of the case, tucked the instrument under her chin and ran the bow across the strings, pausing to tighten the tuning pegs until she was happy with the sound. All the while, she stared at that one man in the audience. She was pleased to see that he'd started to sweat even before she began playing.

The stranger was clearly an accomplished musician, and the unfamiliar melody she played was, they later agreed, oddly compelling—especially to the man with the thick, muscular neck, the man she'd been watching so closely.

After the violinist had finished playing, she offered a hint of a smile to the audience, not so much as a courtesy, but more to stall for just the tiniest bit more time while the apparent man of her dreams slowly stood up, knocking his chair sideways as he did.

The stranger sighed inwardly with desperate relief as she saw him making his way toward her. He was well under her spell. Her great longing would soon be fulfilled. She moved toward him and he moved toward her. Then they made their way together to the edge of the woods, where the shadows would keep her secret.

The other campers were too busy tidying up and herding children into their beds to notice the two who had slipped away—until, that is, a deep-throated scream pierced the air and the muscular tattooed man with the thick neck ran from the woods, his left hand pressed against his neck. Everyone ran toward him to see what the matter was.

And so it was that no one saw the stranger who had played the peculiar tune on her violin make her way back to her camper van. Nor did they see her lick her lips before violently shaking her head, and they certainly didn't see the drops of blood that flew from her mouth with each shaking. Nor did anyone notice when the old camper van drove quietly away. No, no one saw any of that. As a matter of fact, they'd all but forgotten the young woman in the van because they were all focused on the muscular man with the armful of tattoos. He was still screaming in pain. When he had calmed down a little, they could see he was badly injured.

They figured a pair of vicious insects must have attacked him, because there were two holes in his neck. Whatever had bitten him had not only pierced the skin but had gone into the thick, ropy muscles too. It was clear from how dazed and confused the man was that he had lost a considerable amount of blood.

Some of the concerned campers held bandages against his wounds while others went in search of medical help. As the man slipped in and out of consciousness, he writhed in pain and muttered nonsensically something about "her teeth."

A retired doctor who had a trailer parked nearby rushed to the man's side. He dressed the wounds and recommended that the man rest for at least a few days.

The medical attention was obviously sufficient, because a couple of weeks after the incident, he was back at the gym lifting weights. He never spoke of the incident in the woods that summer, but for the rest of his life, he had an aversion to violin music and never went outside when a full moon hung in a clear sky.

GHOST HILL

Not far from Hull, Quebec, in the picturesque Gatineau Hills, is a rural area known as Luskville. Dotted with waterfalls, creeks, and streams, it's a popular place for hiking and trail-walking. Sounds like an idyllic setting, doesn't it? Well, it is, especially for those of us who love a good ghost story, or even several good ghost stories, all in one place. That place is known as Ghost Hill.

There's a road now that runs through Ghost Hill, but if you're planning to drive the route, be sure to keep your wits about you, because there are some steep, sharp turns. There is also said to be a gaggle of ghosts in those hills.

As far as anyone knows, the haunting began way back in the 1800s, when a man named Clyde went out hunting for small game, which was plentiful in the area. He had his trusty rifle with him, and he was a good shot. He smiled to himself as he anticipated the sight of his family sitting down to a good meal of fresh pheasant.

Clyde walked quietly through the bush until he saw a movement in the periphery of his vision. He raised his rifle to his shoulder and took aim. Then he stopped. The animal he heard moving was certainly not small game—it was a cow! He wouldn't want to kill a neighbour's cow. He lowered his gun and started to walk away. When he looked up again, the cow had moved closer to him.

That's the strangest-looking cow I've ever seen, he thought. And that is when the animal charged toward Clyde. He knew he didn't have time to outrun the cow, so he stood his ground, lifted his rifle, and waited until the strange beast was within range. Once it was parallel with a particular tree, he set it in his sight and fired. The animal collapsed against the tree and lay still. Clyde approached slowly. He would have to make sure this peculiar-looking creature was dead. No matter what kind of a cow it was, he didn't want to leave it to die a slow, painful death.

Once he was closer to the prone body, Clyde could see that this was not a cow at all. It was a man covered in a cow's hide. In an instant, Clyde realized that what he had killed was not an animal but his best friend. Clyde crumpled to the ground under the tree next to the body, and that is where some local men found him. They were horrified to see what had happened, especially as they knew the tragedy had started out as a practical joke, one they were all involved in. They had found the cow's hide just that day and had drawn straws to decide which one of them would have the fun of scaring Clyde while he was out hunting. The dead man, Walter, had drawn the lethal short straw.

None of their lives were ever the same after that, and the poor deceased's afterlife was as hideous as his death. It's said that his soul attached itself to the tree where he died, and that theory seemed to have some grounding, because over time, the tree took on an eerie appearance, as though its branches were arms, with twigs looking like fingers. Even its roots looked like knees. The worst part, though, was that over the years, one side of the tree trunk, the side where Walter's lifeless body had lain, took on the appearance of a wrinkled old man's face.

People in the area became afraid to go near that tree. Some claimed that their wagon wheels wouldn't turn as they passed the tree, forcing them to jump from the wagon and flee, leaving their horses neighing and pawing at the ground as though some invisible force was terrorizing them. Others said they heard inexplicable moans and groans coming from the tree. Soon the place became known as Ghost Hill, and no one would go near it.

Joseph Lusk owned the property where the unnatural tree stood. He decided that the only solution was to cut the tree down. That was a brave thought indeed, but when it came time to swing his axe to the trunk, Joseph was not so brave. They say he cried out like a man possessed as he hacked away at the base of the tree. Before he was finished, a storm blew across Lusk's property, lashing bolts of lightning at the man. But he kept at his task, all the while hearing screams echoing around him. Finally he stood surrounded by nothing more than wood chips. He had succeeded in slaying the evil, but to his dying day, Lusk maintained that with each swing of the axe, he felt as though he was cutting into a human being.

Despite the dreadful emotional price he paid, at least his property was no longer haunted. Or so he thought, until the evening when two friends were walking home through the woods from the local pub. Just as they were approaching Ghost

Hill, they began to argue about some inconsequential matter. Their beer-fuelled altercation ended with one of the men dead—at the very top of Ghost Hill. It's said that to this day, his spirit haunts that hill.

Soon people with common sense began avoiding the locale—except for a man named Jim Boyer. One day, he had been at the tavern celebrating a successful day selling his goods at the market, and the beer he celebrated with had washed away every ounce of common sense he might have had. Robbers found him staggering around near Ghost Hill. He was an easy target, so they shoved him to the ground and stole the profits he still had. Then they left him to die, and Boyer's soul joined the other presences on the hill.

Some people believe that these men's spirits haunt the area to this day, and those folks just might be correct. Even in modern times, there have been terrible car accidents on the road that now runs through the land once owned by Joseph Lusk. Those accidents have officially been blamed on drivers not being careful enough on the road's sharp turn and steep hill.

That explanation didn't offer a particular bus driver any peace of mind, though. He thought he was driving an empty bus through the pretty area, but when he looked in his mirror, he saw an old woman sitting quietly in one of the seats. She held her handbag in her lap and was gazing out at the countryside as the bus chugged its way along.

A few minutes later, the driver heard what sounded like a gust of wind. When he looked around, the bus was as empty as he'd thought it had been earlier; the old woman had vanished. Shocked, he stopped the bus and walked to the back where the woman had been sitting. There was no one there. The poor man was in such a state that he had to get out of the bus and get some fresh air to settle himself. That's when he noticed a small cemetery located where he had heard the gust of wind, just before he noticed that his eerie passenger was gone. It would've been understandable if he'd decided to choose another career after that day!

These stories are how Ghost Hill earned its name. Perhaps these legends that haunt the hill should serve as cautionary tales to remind us to have reverence for human life.

A COLD THANKSGIVING

Older people sometimes like to think that only youngsters can get themselves in trouble by not being careful enough, but that's not always true. One Thanksgiving Day weekend, Steve Taylor was staying alone at his cottage on Lake Manitoba. He was there to close the place down for the year and also to receive the new boat he'd bought at a yard sale. Steve hadn't really wanted to buy this boat, but it was smaller and lighter than his old one, and his arms had weakened so much over the years that his old boat was getting too much for him to manage.

Steve had owned the cottage for most of his adult life and, over the years, he and his family had enjoyed their summers at the lake, where they'd made lots of friends. But this week-end, all their neighbours were back in the city, enjoying turkey dinner with their families. Steve wished someone else was around so he could show off his new boat, but even if there wasn't, it would be fun to take it out on the water just to see how it handled.

The sun was low in the sky as Steve pushed off from the dock. He manoeuvred the boat hesitantly at first, but once he became comfortable with how it responded, he thrust the throttle forward. Boating had always been one of Steve's great pleasures, so he was grateful that his days on the water weren't over. This little craft was just a pleasure to pilot through the water.

Peppy too, he thought. *I'm already out in the middle of the lake.*

Exhilarated, he complimented himself on the wisdom of his purchase—until the engine stuttered. And then stopped completely.

Those cheapskates who sold me this boat didn't even leave me with a full tank of gas, he muttered angrily to himself. *There should be a spare tank, though.*

He lifted a hatch and, sure enough, there was the spare— and judging by the weight of the tank, it was full. The trouble was, Steve's arms weren't strong enough to heft the container close enough to the engine to hook up the lines.

Steve looked around him. The sky was darkening quickly, and there were no lights on in any of the cabins around the lake. Steve was in serious trouble, and he knew it. He looked around for flares, or even oars, but there were none. Frustratingly, there was an anchor but no rope. There was nothing he could do but drift.

And drift he did. Soon it was pitch-dark, and a nasty wind blew up. He lay on the bottom of the boat to keep out of the wind. "I was so cold," he remembered later. "All I had for a cover were two life jackets. I draped one over my chest and one across my knees, but they really weren't much help."

By then, Steve's body was shaking with both fear and cold. He was utterly helpless. Eventually, the boat beached itself with a crunch on a shoal. He stepped out onto the sand, but his eyes couldn't penetrate the darkness. As he climbed back into the boat, his foot caught on something and he fell against the far side. *You'll have some bruises, you silly old fool, but at least nothing's broken*, he thought. *And what the dickens did I catch my foot on?*

Steve couldn't believe his eyes—a searchlight! The new boat had come equipped with a huge searchlight.

"I flashed SOS around all over the place, but there was no one there to see my signal," Steve later recalled.

Steve knew his situation was grim. Not only was he totally alone, but he was also dangerously cold and weak with hunger. Every circumstance was conspiring against the odds of him coming through this misadventure alive.

"Then, God bless it, it started to snow," he recalled. "I ate the snow. It helped to keep me alive, but it didn't snow very long and so when it stopped falling, I staggered out of the boat and over to the edge of the lake and drank that."

Meanwhile, hypothermia was creeping through his body.

"Maybe I was hallucinating, but the Devil appeared before me. He grinned and said, 'I've got you now.'"

As emphatically and colourfully as he could, Steve told the Devil to leave. "I was rather rude," he acknowledged later.

"I want to talk to God," he told the Devil before imploring God's help directly. "I said, 'God, where are you when I need you?'"

The only sound Steve heard were the waves lapping up on the shore.

"Then, way off in the distance, I heard a husky voice say, 'Have faith and keep trying.'"

There was something familiar about the voice. *I must have lost my mind*, Steve thought. *That sounds like a woman's voice.*

The air around him grew colder, and the air pressure seemed to increase. Steve knew his circumstances were dire. "Have faith, keep trying," the voice repeated. So familiar; that voice was so familiar, but his addled brain was beyond making any connections.

Shaking from cold and fear, he mustered what little strength he had left and answered the phantom voice. "That's good advice, but who's going to fix these weak arms of mine?"

He lay in the boat, praying that someone would come along—all the while hearing the husky voice echoing in his head: "Have faith, keep trying."

Whenever he could summon the energy, Steve called out for help, but there was no one to hear his pleas. Eventually, he realized that his only alternative to waiting for imminent death was to follow the advice of the ethereal voice. He had to have faith that he would make it through the terrible ordeal alive. He had to keep trying.

Slowly, the veracity of those haunting words worked their way into his mind. He had to attempt what he thought was impossible. "I grasped the spare tank with all the strength I could muster. Little by little, I managed to move the tank close enough to hook it up."

"Finally, I turned the key in the ignition. It started!"

Steve didn't let his hopes get too high, though, because he was still grounded on the shoal.

"I tried to ease the boat out of there—backward and forward, backward and forward. All I could hear was *crunch, crunch, bang, bang.*"

More determined than ever to heed the disembodied voice, he reasoned that there had to be some way to escape the complexity of this apparent deathtrap.

"The boat was at a precarious angle. I needed to see just which rocks were holding me back. There was a huge boulder right beside the propeller, and I thought if I wheeled the motor around full to the right and backed it up, I might just scrape by. I tried that, and the propellers went *crash, bang, crash, bang,* and then suddenly all was quiet. I was moving! I got off the shoal, the boat was floating, and the motor was running—but I wasn't sure where I was. I headed in what I thought was a southeasterly direction. It was so cold, and it seemed like it would start snowing again. I managed to avoid a cluster of shoals and finally spotted a familiar cottage, one that's not far from ours. I had been at least ten kilometres from home. I'd drifted that far."

Steve made it home safely that night, all the while crediting that unseen presence and its voice with his rescue. Had he not heard those words of encouragement over and over again, he might not have persisted with the necessary determination to save himself. As it was, he barely made it into his boathouse. Fortunately, his all-terrain vehicle was there for him to drive up the hill to the life-giving warmth of his cottage. Once safely inside, Steve made himself a pot of strong tea and a serving of warm soup before crawling into bed and sleeping straight through for fourteen hours.

When he finally woke up, he phoned his daughter, who immediately drove to the cottage and took her father to get a medical exam.

The doctor, a man about Steve's own age, commented, "I'd say you've come as close to hell as you're going to without going in."

Steve didn't bother to tell the doctor about his run-in with the Devil.

Driving home, though, he decided that he could tell his daughter about the hallucination and the inexplicable gravelly voice urging him to have faith and keep trying. He laughed mirthlessly in an attempt to make light of the uncomfortable situation. "I called out to God for help, but the voice that answered was quite a shock."

"Why's that?" his daughter queried.

"Because I didn't know that God sounded like a woman who'd smoked a pack of cigarettes every day of her life."

Steve's daughter was quiet for a moment. Then she said, "Dad, that wasn't God. That was Grandma—your mother. She had a raspy voice from smoking."

Steve was silent for a moment and then said quietly, "You're right."

A moment later he added, "I guess I'll have to rethink a few of my beliefs."

"While you're at it, have a little talk with yourself about safety, too, Dad. Next time you need her, Grandma might be out for a heavenly smoke break."

SOMETHING IN COMMON

Clark's sneakers crunched across the gravel parking lot to the all-night restaurant. He was hungry and badly needed a break from driving. He hugged his arms around himself, sorry that he hadn't worn his parka. When he'd left Lac La Ronge it had been a warm afternoon, but this was the last day of the Labour Day weekend, and he knew all too well that in northern Saskatchewan, the weather could change in the time it took to snap his fingers.

He pulled open the restaurant door and was immediately welcomed with warmth and the delicious smells of baked goods.

The waitress waved him in, saying, "Give that door a good hard tug, will you, son? The wind is so bad it's been catching and blowing open every so often. Last thing we need is to have the door ripped off."

Clark nodded and did as he was told before wiping the gravel off the soles of his shoes. He looked around for a place to sit down. The tables scattered about the room were all occupied by truckers hunched over steaming cups of coffee, so he gave one of the stools at the counter a twirl before sitting down on it.

"Just coffee?" the waitress asked as she gave the counter in front of him a cursory wipe.

"I think I'd better have a sandwich, too, if you have one ready."

"Ham and cheese all right? It's all we have left."

Clark nodded absently, his mind already on the decision he knew he had to make quickly. He cleared his throat and called out to no one in particular, "Excuse me. Does anyone know what the roads are like to the south?"

A few men grunted ambiguously. Others said nothing before resuming whatever conversation Clark's question had interrupted.

Hearing that her customer wasn't getting the information he needed and considering the storm howling outside, the waitress turned from the grill she'd been scraping. She said to Clark, "A trucker who stopped in on his way northbound told me that the roads south of Prince Albert were good, but between here and there, he said there's snow and ice."

Clark mumbled his thanks, still not sure what to do. He badly needed to be back at work in Prince Albert the next morning. He'd messed up way too many times as far as his boss was concerned. If his job wasn't on the line already, then it was getting close, and not showing up could easily mean the end. Still, without the proper gear, hitting a patch of ice and skidding into a ditch could be fatal, especially when you were by yourself.

He paid for his food and left the warmth and protection of the restaurant. He needed to think about what to do. He'd seen a little old rundown motel just behind the restaurant, so that was an option; but there was his job to consider.

The moment he set foot outside the door, he was forcibly reminded of just how severe the storm was. A freezing cold wind whipped clouds of snow crystals into swirls.

Not good, he thought. *I'll get my wallet from the car and check into the motel. If I end up unemployed, so be it. Better than ending up dead.*

Relieved that he'd made his decision, Clark walked toward the passenger side of his car to retrieve his wallet from the glove compartment. As he approached, he was stopped in his tracks by the realization of how bad the visibility really was. Why, it actually looked as though there was someone standing beside his car.

Clark blinked his eyes, but the vision beside the car didn't vanish.

He jumped when the indistinct figure called out, "Hello."

"What the . . . ?" Clark muttered, his fists tightening reflexively. "Who are you? What are you doing beside my car?"

"Sorry, I didn't mean to startle you. I'm harmless, honest. I'm looking for a ride south toward Prince Albert. Are you going that way?"

Clark's heart was still thumping hard enough from the surprise of finding the man standing out in the storm beside his car that it took him a minute to consider his answer—which gave the stranger time to add that he had a cell phone with him in case they had any trouble.

Relief washed over Clark. How could he be so lucky? He'd get home tonight and get to work tomorrow. "I am heading south, and I'd be really glad to have some company for the drive," he said. "By the way, I'm Clark. What's your name?"

"Robert," the man answered as he finished scraping ice that had accumulated on the car windows.

"Do folks call you Rob or Robbie or Bob or something?" Clark asked, just to make conversation as he steered the car out onto the dark highway.

"No, I go by Robert," the young man answered. "It's sort of a nickname as it is. My first name is actually Robertson. It was my mother's name before she married my dad."

"Really?" Clark asked with genuine surprise. "That's a weird coincidence. My name is my mother's maiden name too."

The man in the passenger seat only nodded. He appeared to be drifting off to sleep. Clark took the opportunity to eyeball the man a bit more closely. They looked to be about the same age and even much the same height and build. *I wonder what the guy does for a living. And why the heck was he out on the highway in the middle of nowhere tonight?*

He couldn't spend too much time sneaking looks at his companion or even too many seconds wondering about him, because he needed to focus on the road ahead. Without a doubt, the driving conditions were getting worse.

And that wasn't Clark's only problem. The combination of the stressful driving conditions and the sandwich back at the truck stop hadn't agreed with his stomach. *I need a roll of antacids,* he thought. He glanced over at his passenger and felt a pang of envy. The guy had been in a dead sleep pretty much the whole time. *Okay, next exit, I'll pull off. I just hope I don't have to drive too far into a town to find a store that's open late.*

A faint yellow puddle of light in the distance gave Clark hope that he'd soon be chewing an antacid tablet or two and that the roads south of Prince Albert had remained in better shape than the ones he'd just driven over. His passenger was so deeply asleep by now that he was snoring noisily.

Clark pulled up in front of a convenience store and turned off the car's ignition, hoping that the change in noise and vibration would wake Robert; he could do with the company. But Robert continued to sleep peacefully. *I'll just leave him, I guess,* Clark thought, but as a precaution, he took the key out of the ignition and tucked it into his jeans' pocket. By the time he came out of the store just a few minutes later, Clark decided that he'd been paranoid and unkind in turning off the car. The guy had given no indication he was anything but a straight shooter. Taking the keys really was a bit of an insult. *If he's awake, I'll tell him sorry, that it was just habit.*

But Clark never had the opportunity to apologize, because by the time he got back to his car, the passenger seat was empty.

"Robert!" he called, thinking that the man must be nearby, stretching his legs and getting some fresh air. The only answer was the whine of the wind through the sentinel of pine trees behind the store.

"Well, that's inconsiderate of him," Clark muttered to himself as he made his way back to the store, now figuring that Robert had gone inside and that the two had somehow missed seeing one another.

But when he asked him, the man behind the counter shook his head. "You're the only one who's come in here for more than an hour, son. If I see him, though, I'll let him know you waited a bit for him."

Clark nodded and made his way back toward his car. Robert was still nowhere to be seen, and Clark was surprised at how sorry he was that he'd apparently be making this last leg of the trip on his own once again, even if the storm had let up considerably and the road looked to be in much better condition. He backed out of his parking spot, changed from reverse to drive—and slammed on the brake. The only footprints in the parking lot were his own. The snow on the passenger's side of the car was thick and deep and completely unmarked—not a footprint in sight. Robert hadn't gotten out of the car so much as he had simply vanished from the car. Then Clark noticed that Robert's parka lay on the car seat, his cell phone on top of that.

This is freakin' impossible, Clark thought, slamming the car door and stumbling toward the store again.

"What's going on here?" he asked the storekeeper, his voice shaking.

"I can't honestly say I know, son, except to tell you that stuff like this has been happening since even before the time I owned this store. I don't rightly know if it's some kind of altered time/space continuum, or a ghost, or a guardian angel, or quite what's at work here."

"So, you've seen this guy Robertson before?"

The man sighed. "I don't know what to tell you. No, I've never seen him. It's an odd thing. I know about him, or them, or it, or whatever the right term should be. It always happens on this stretch of road, and whoever or whatever it is always has something in common with the person who's picked them up. Sometimes it's a man, sometimes a woman. It seems to depend on who the driver is that needs help. It usually happens in the winter, probably just because the roads are the worst then, but once in June a woman came in here all upset. She was diabetic and had neglected to eat before she left. Then some other woman flagged her down just a few kilometres along and asked for a ride. First thing she pulled out of her purse was a full bottle of orange juice. She said that she didn't want it, something about it not being the brand she liked. It was exactly what the driver needed, just a bit of nourishment to tide her over. They pulled in here so the driver could buy some juice that was more to the other lady's liking. But when she got back to the car, the passenger's seat was empty except for the juice bottle."

Clark shook his head, not wanting to believe either the experience he'd just had or the story he'd just heard. He thanked the man and walked back through the snow to the car. There on the passenger's seat still lay the parka that Robertson had been wearing, with the cell phone on top. He knew he had everything he needed to make the rest of the trip in safety.

What he didn't know was what he'd do if that cell phone ever rang.

*

DANCE HALL VISION

Adam and Aaron were identical twin brothers. All their lives, they'd had fun fooling people with which one was which. There were times, though, that their individual identities were important to them, and this particular summer evening— August 21—was one of those times.

They'd been visiting their parents at the family cabin in rural New Brunswick, and when Saturday evening rolled around, they decided to take the boat over to the community wharf and check out the dance hall out on the pier.

"Have the boat home by ten," their father told them.

Their mother added, "In other words, don't be out on the lake after dark."

"Same diff," their father grumbled.

Adam laughed as he grabbed his denim jacket from a hook by the door and waited while Aaron pulled a blue sweater over his head. The boys were in their late teens now and well used to their mother and father's different parenting styles. They also knew that their father would be asleep in his recliner well before ten and that if they were a bit late, their mother wouldn't give them any grief.

While one brother untied the boat's ropes from the dock, the other started the engine. The lake was as calm as glass. They took the long route to the dance hall in order to go past friends' cabins and see who was up at the lake and who hadn't arrived from the city yet. Over the years, they'd made so many good friends during their summers at the lake.

"Looks like almost everyone's here this weekend," Adam shouted to Aaron over the roar of the boat's motor, but Aaron just smiled and nodded with a faraway look in his eyes. Adam had no way of knowing that his identical twin brother had just been hit by a feeling that something good—really good—was about to happen.

The boys docked the boat, and Adam jumped out to tie the ropes to the bollards on the wharf. Aaron, meanwhile, was still in the boat and seemed to be staring off into space. Adam looked around to follow his brother's gaze and saw a beautiful young woman walking toward the dance hall. He knew the sort of girl his brother was attracted to, and this one had it all. She was tall and slight, with thick curls of red hair. When she walked, it was like poetry in motion.

"I'm calling dibs," Aaron said with no hint of teasing in his voice.

"Figured you would," Adam said with a chuckle.

When he heard the band start to play, Aaron nearly ran into the hall. He just didn't want to take any chances that some other guy might ask her to dance before he did. Then he paused at the door. After all, he didn't want the girl to think that he was running up to attack her. Besides, it was darker inside than out, and at first, he couldn't even spot her.

As his eyes adjusted to the dim light, he scanned the room again; still no redhead. *Maybe she's in the washroom,* he thought. Then, on his third scan, there she was, standing in a shadow in the far corner of the room—no wonder he hadn't been able to see her.

As the band eased in to the next dance tune, Aaron walked slowly but determinedly toward the vision of loveliness who had stolen his heart.

"Hello," he said. "My name is Aaron. Will you dance with me?"

For a moment, she didn't respond. Aaron held his breath. She was even more beautiful up close than she had been from afar. Her skin was so pure and white that it was almost translucent. He could feel his heart thumping in his chest.

Finally she replied, "I'd like that very much. My name is Annalee."

Together, the two danced the night away.

So this is what love feels like, Aaron thought dreamily.

During the band's break, he asked if she'd like to go somewhere for a warm drink. "You must be cold," he said. "Your skin feels chilly."

"I'd like that very much, but I'd better not. I need to be getting home. My parents worry if I'm late."

Aaron began to feel something close to panic. He couldn't take a chance on losing her before they even got to know one another. "May I take you home, then? My brother and I have our boat here. It wouldn't take a minute. We'd be happy to do that. We need to leave pretty soon, too." He could hear himself chattering on like a fool, but he was desperate not to let the girl of his dreams slip away.

"No, thank you. I have my rowboat here," she replied.

"Let me walk you to the wharf, then," he pleaded.

"I'll be fine," she said quietly and gave him a kiss on the right cheek. The touch of her lips against his skin felt like dry ice burning his cheek.

"I'd like to see you again," Aaron declared.

"Oh, you will," Annalee said before disappearing into the crowd and out of the hall.

Aaron leaned against a pillar waiting for his head to stop spinning. A second later, Adam approached him and gave his lovestruck brother a fist bump on the shoulder.

"I was keeping an eye on you there, fella," he said, but Aaron didn't react. He just kept leaning on the pillar with his eyes unfocused. "Come on. Let's go. We need to get home."

Aaron nodded, and the two made their way to the wharf, untied their boat, and jumped in.

"I'm driving," Adam said. "You're sure in no condition to handle a boat safely."

Aaron didn't reply.

As they crossed the lake, their boat's engine thrummed a steady rhythm that Aaron, in his dreamy state, found hypnotic. Then, in a heartbeat, he jumped up from where he had been sitting in the moving boat. "Stop, Adam, stop!" he screamed, waving his arms to get his brother's attention.

"Have you gone insane?" Adam screamed back at him. "Sit down!"

"Look!" Aaron replied, gesturing to a point in the water about ten metres off their starboard side.

Adam turned the boat around slightly so its light was shining at the spot Aaron was pointing to. There, in the water, was a small overturned rowboat.

"Help me!" a tired-sounding voice called.

Adam cut the engine. He and Aaron each grabbed a paddle and manoeuvred the boat toward the person in the water who was so obviously in serious distress. As they drew alongside, Aaron's heart rose to his throat. It was her, Annalee, the girl he'd been dancing with all night! He pulled off his shoes and sweater before jumping into the lake.

"I've got you, I've got you," he assured the struggling girl, and a moment later, he lifted her slight form from the water and safely into their boat. While Adam went back to the bow of the boat, Aaron stayed in the stern and slipped his blue sweater over Annalee's cold, wet shoulders.

"Where's your cottage?" Adam asked her.

She pointed to the far shore, and he turned the boat in that direction.

Aaron sat with his arm around his beautiful dance partner, partly to share his body heat with her but mostly because he was sure, by now, that he was in love with her. As he held her, though, she began shivering.

"Were you frightened?" he asked her.

"Very," she said.

Then Aaron made his way up toward the front of the boat and asked his brother to slow down because he was scaring the girl by driving too fast.

By the time he crawled back to the stern of the boat, Annalee was gone.

"What?" Aaron shrieked.

Adam turned around and saw that he and his brother were alone in the boat. "Oh my God! What should we do?" Adam called out.

"What if she fell overboard? I'm going into the water to see if I can find her," said Aaron as he once again plunged into the lake.

But the water was too dark for him to even see his hand in front of his face. He climbed back into the boat.

"She was pointing to that cottage," he said. "That must be where she lives. We'll have to go there and tell them what's happened."

Adam steered the boat toward the light on the shore while Aaron huddled against the gunwales as best as he could. His body shook from cold and fear.

As they docked the boat, an elderly couple walked down a set of wooden stairs and came out on the dock to meet them.

Aaron tried to speak, but he was shivering so badly that he was incoherent. Adam managed to at least introduce himself and his brother to the couple.

"You don't have to tell us," the man said. "We know exactly what happened."

The man's wife added, "We're the Millers, and we've been expecting you."

"Well, not necessarily you two, but we knew someone would show up at our dock just after ten o'clock," the man continued.

"You see, it's the anniversary. Every August someone sees our daughter at the dance hall, but it's not real. Many years ago, she did go to the hall to attend a dance, but her little rowboat overturned that night as she made her way home. The people who see her always try to help her, but sadly, they fail," the old woman explained with tears in her eyes.

"It's been forty years now. We thought it would have stopped by now, but apparently not. We do appreciate your efforts, though, boys," the man assured them. Adam and Aaron stood utterly speechless.

Finally, the two young men made their way back to their boat. Adam waved to the elderly couple and they waved back at him. Aaron just sat as his brother propelled the boat back to their cottage, where they knew their father would be asleep in his recliner and their mother would be waiting up for them. They had quite a story for her.

The brothers tied up the boat and had started to walk up the hill to the cabin when Adam noticed that Aaron had left his sweater in the boat. Adam went back to pick it up and then handed the wet garment to his twin. "You must've had that on when you went into the water to look for Annalee," he said.

Aaron shook his head but said nothing.

Half an hour later, he had changed into warm, dry clothing and was sitting at the dining room table with his mother and brother.

"Have you ever met the Millers? They have a cottage on the other side of the lake," Adam said.

"They used to, you mean. It was an awful thing. Their daughter drowned when a powerboat sped by her and swamped her little rowboat. She was on her way home from a dance about ten o'clock one Saturday night in August. But that was years ago. Her parents, the Millers, left the cottage the next day and never came back. For years it sat empty, exactly as they had left it. The beds were still made, and there was still food in the cupboards. It even looked as though they'd prepared hot cocoa for their daughter to have when she got home that night. Of course, she never did. So sad," their mother concluded.

"Awful," was all Adam could think of to say.

Aaron shuddered.

After that, people who looked closely enough could always tell Adam from Aaron because, on his right cheek, Aaron had a small scar, as if he'd been burned by dry ice. The mark was just the size and shape of a girl's lips.

EXTRATERRESTRIAL VISIT

It was dusk when Judd was walking along the deserted roadway leading from the outskirts of Brandon, Manitoba, into the city. If you'd seen him, you might have guessed that he was dejected, especially if you knew he'd just sold the only car he'd ever owned, but Judd wasn't unhappy at all. Tonight was his last night in civvy street. He had joined the army and was due to report for his first day of basic training the next morning. The sun would be setting in about an hour, and he just wanted to enjoy a leisurely stroll for the last time. After this, he'd be marching, possibly at double time, or running, wherever he went.

A wind blew up, which didn't surprise Judd; after all, this was the Prairies in summer. It had been hot enough through the day that there might even be a thunderstorm brewing. He did hope that he was home before that hit, if it did. For now, though, the wind had just brought a heavy bank of clouds that hid the sun and darkened the sky. The young man decided that he should probably hitchhike the rest of the way back into town. In the meantime, he'd keep walking, even quickening his pace. If he heard a car coming his way, though, he'd stick out his thumb.

But there were no cars on the road going in either direction, and by now, Judd was starting to worry. He could feel the electric tang in the air that all Prairie kids recognize as the forerunner to a doozy of a thunderstorm. He'd be a sitting duck for a lightning strike out there alone on the road. He willed a car or a truck to come along and pick him up, but his mind trick didn't work.

The wind died down, leaving only the heavy cloud cover. *This must be the calm before the storm,* he thought, growing more and more uneasy. He looked around for shelter, but there were empty fields as far as the eye could see. The utter silence set his nerves on edge. There was nothing he could do but keep walking as quickly as he could, because the world around him was now as dark as night. At least he wasn't in any imminent danger, or so he hoped.

Something on the horizon caught Judd's eye: two small lights, some distance apart. *Those must be farmhouses,* he thought with relief. He could take refuge there if the storm started. Then he saw a third light, this one in the sky. He stared in disbelief as an enormous, brightly glowing circular object flew across the dark sky. The thing was huge, and it was headed directly toward him.

Judd jumped for the drainage ditch at the side of the road. Crouched in the stagnant water, he watched this strange craft follow him and hover just above his wet, shivering body.

Then, after a time, the object silently floated away, disappearing in the blink of an eye. Terrified, Judd stood up, and the putrid ditch water drained from his clothes. He ran as fast as he could toward the light he had seen in the farmhouse window. A few seconds later, he was pounding on the front door and screaming that he needed help, all the while furtively checking the sky for any sign of the strange, flying circle. Much to his relief, he couldn't see a trace any of it.

Soon it was apparent that whoever was inside the house was not about to open the door to a screaming, door-pounding man, so Judd walked back to the road, praying that he'd get a ride back to town.

When he first saw lights approaching him on the horizon, he nearly jumped in the ditch again; but then he realized that these were car headlights. His rescuers had arrived! He stood in the middle of the road, waving his hands above his head and calling out, "Stop, stop!"

The middle-aged couple driving home after an evening of playing cards with friends got the shock of their lives as the soaking young man told them that he'd been pursued by a flying saucer. Worse still, he wanted to get into their car. Judd could sense their reluctance to give him a ride. He tried to stay calm and asked them to please drop him off at the first police station they came to. They were glad to do that—but nothing more. After dropping him off, they drove away as quickly as possible.

Judd tried to compose himself before telling the desk sergeant that there was a flying saucer cruising the skies around Brandon, but he wasn't entirely successful.

"Well," the Mountie said, "can't say as I've ever heard a story like that before. I'll take your report, though, because that's my job."

Just as they were finishing up the paperwork, a cruiser pulled up in front of the station and a constable made his way into the building.

"What a night," he said, taking off his hat and running his fingers through his hair. "I had some kook of a woman flag me over and give me this cock-and-bull story about seeing a flying saucer."

Judd swung around. "She did?" he asked excitedly.

The constable looked taken aback. "Sorry, sir, I didn't see you there. I spoke out of turn."

"I saw it too!" Judd exclaimed. "What else did she say?"

"I didn't even bother taking notes, because I thought she was just a wing nut. From what I recall, though, she said this round, glowing object was silently flying through the air and that it followed her for several kilometres."

"Then what?" Judd prompted.

"She said it hovered above her car for a while and then disappeared in the blink of an eye."

The desk sergeant cleared his throat. "Do you think that woman saw the same thing as you did?" he asked Judd, who nodded mutely in response.

The policemen looked at each other, and then the desk sergeant said, "Constable, you'd better get back out there and check into this."

The constable asked Judd if he could offer directions as to where he'd seen the mysterious object.

"I'll come with you," Judd said. "I know exactly where I was on the road, because there were two farmhouses off in the distance."

As Judd and the constable headed outside to get into the cruiser, the desk sergeant ordered them to radio in anything unusual. He'd heard rumours that other possible UFO sightings had been reported, but he'd presumed they were just gossip, and nothing had been officially noted.

It was close to three in the morning when Judd and the constable pulled off to the side of the road near the two farmhouses. All was still, on the ground and in the sky. Even so, the two men in the cruiser were tense and on high alert. The constable radioed in, hoping that the sergeant would have them come back to the station. But from the safety of the chair behind his desk, the senior man decided that there should be some further investigation. "Get your flashlights and walk around a bit. See if you can spot anything out of the ordinary."

Judd and the constable climbed out of the police car and walked across a farmer's field. They could hear a horse neighing excitedly and stomping its hooves. Then a dog started to howl. Could the animals be sensing something that the humans weren't able to?

Judd looked up and examined the sky carefully. Suddenly he shouted, "I see it! I see it!"

The constable looked up. He could barely believe his eyes. There, above a copse of trees in the distance, was a round, glowing object in the sky. And it was coming toward them. The men were blinded by the light the object was emitting.

"That thing's twice as big as both of those houses," the constable said, his voice shaking in fear and disbelief.

They watched, paralyzed by fear and awe as the silent, lighted craft began to flash red lights at them. The red lights grew dimmer and then suddenly glowed so brightly that the whole countryside was glowing blood-red, illuminating both farmhouses and all the land around them.

Judd and the constable made a dash for the relative safety of the police cruiser. The object in the sky followed them and then hovered over the car for a time. The constable turned the key in the ignition, but the engine was dead. All was still and quiet.

The constable grabbed the radio's mic and shouted to the sergeant, "I can see the thing myself!"

Moments later, a second police cruiser pulled up. He had been monitoring the calls on the radio and had raced to the scene to see if he could help.

The object was still visible, hovering over the trees as it glowed iridescently and flashed the red lights rhythmically. Then, in a heartbeat, it was gone, heading west across the prairies. The horses stopped neighing and stomping. The dogs stopped howling and barking. The field was dark and still. All had returned to normal. The encounter was over.

What had happened that quiet summer's night on the outskirts of Brandon? Had they seen a UFO? Were there intelligent beings from another planet inside?

All Judd knew was that adrenaline alone would have to take him through his first day of military life and that he certainly had a story to tell the boys in the barracks.

STORIES BY CANDLELIGHT

AN UNSOLVED MYSTERY

Sailing a ship across the frigid waters of the Atlantic Ocean in the nineteenth century was a tough job that required tough sailors, and the captains of those ships had to be even tougher. Many captains were so tough that they had lost every shred of humanity they ever had. When that was the case, the only thing left that mattered was completing the voyage alive and making a profit—any way they could.

A man named Baker was the captain of the *Ellen Austin*. She had set sail from England and was nearing her destination of St. John's, Newfoundland, when her crew sighted an unidentified schooner drifting aimlessly in the water nearby. Baker ordered the lookout to call to those aboard the unidentified ship. There was no reply.

Baker ordered his ship to make its way closer to the mystery vessel so that he could get a better look. When they were closer, he hailed the captain, but only the sound of his own voice echoed back at them. He brought the *Ellen Austin* closer still and commandeered four of his sailors. Together, they launched a small boat and rowed to the schooner. The five men boarded the mysterious vessel with their weapons drawn.

Once they were on board, the curious men searched the ship from stem to gudgeon. Everything on board was in—well, shipshape condition. There were no signs that there had been violence or even a struggle onboard. The bunks were all neatly made, and the mess was well provisioned. But there wasn't a soul on board other than themselves.

Strangely, though, the schooner's nameplates had been removed and her logbook was missing from the captain's cabin.

By now the sailors from the *Ellen Austin* had lost their curiosity and wanted nothing more than to flee from this unnatural ship. Even Captain Baker was uneasy, but he knew that salvaging the abandoned craft would be highly profitable, so he set up a new logbook and, under the day's date, noted that his crew had taken over the abandoned craft. He ordered the four men who had accompanied him to stay aboard and sail the craft into St. John's, following his ship, until they had docked at the harbour so there could be no question of who was owed the salvage proceeds.

The first day, the skeleton crew in the nameless schooner was able to keep pace behind the leading ship, but that night a violent storm crossed the paths of the ships. High winds and even higher waves forced the ships farther and farther apart until all contact between the two was lost.

By the next morning, the bad weather had passed and the waves calmed. Soon the crew of the *Ellen Austin* spotted the schooner in the distance. Much to Captain Baker's shock, the other vessel appeared to be drifting aimlessly again. For a second time, he ordered his ship to approach the other one. This time the four sailors he chose to accompany him weren't at all curious—they were flat-out terrified, but they knew that disobeying a captain's orders was a serious offence.

What they found on board horrified them. The ship was once again deserted, and the new logbook had vanished—but nothing else appeared to have been touched.

Despite having no idea what fate had befallen the first four members of his crew, Captain Baker ordered this second group of four to stay on board the schooner. The men begged not to be left behind on the mysterious ship, but in the end, they had no choice but to obey orders.

Soon, another North Atlantic storm blew up. The lookout manning the *Ellen Austin* did everything he could to keep his trailing shipmates in sight, but it was hopeless. The weather was so bad that he could barely see his hand in front of his face. By then, even Captain Baker knew he was dealing with forces well beyond his own. He ordered his ship to sail for St. John's as quickly as possible.

And that, for the captain and the remaining crew of the *Ellen Austin*, was the end of the story. Until their dying days, not one of them ever saw those eight shipmates or the mystery schooner again.

But others have.

Hikers along Newfoundland's beautiful rugged east coast occasionally report seeing an old-fashioned schooner drifting aimlessly out in the ocean. Then, when they look again, a fog bank has rolled in and the ship is nowhere to be seen.

GRAVE CALL

You wouldn't recognize the place now, but fifty years ago, the community of MacTier, near Georgian Bay in Ontario's cottage country, was barely even a sleepy hamlet. Some of the houses were tiny cabins with dirt floors and outdoor plumbing. But even then, one particular house had all the modern conveniences: hot and cold running water, electricity, and even a telephone.

Identical twins Dyllis and Phyllis had inherited this lovely home from their uncle, who had raised them. The twins were apparently so content with their lot in life and each other's company that they didn't venture out very much. When their neighbours saw them in town, the two would smile and nod and perhaps pass the time of day with a bit of conversation, but that was about all. Neither, it seemed, had ever had a suitor, and no one was ever invited into their home.

Every month when the two would pay their telephone bill, Stella, the woman who ran the post office, wondered why they bothered with a phone, but of course, she didn't ever say anything about it—well, not to Phyllis and Dyllis, that is. She certainly made lots of comments about it to everyone else in

120

town. But mostly the townsfolk just accepted that the sisters were odd ducks, and everyone went happily on with their lives.

As the years went by, generations of children grew up and had children of their own. Folks from the city came to the area and built cottages the size of palaces, but life for the twins didn't change one bit. In fine weather, they would sit out in their back garden, and in winter, they stayed inside, reading books they had borrowed from the local library.

Then, one early spring day, one of the twins—no one could ever tell them apart—came running out of the house screaming hysterically. She was so upset that the first person to get to her couldn't understand what she was saying. Fortunately, the second person to arrive on the scene went straight into the house and found Phyllis—lying unconscious on the floor. That might have been the first time the twins' phone had been used since their uncle had died, but it was certainly useful that day, because it meant that the ambulance got there in a matter of minutes.

Despite the prompt medical attention, Phyllis died a few minutes later. When the local undertaker arrived, Dyllis was very clear about how the funeral would be handled. She politely declined floral tributes and made it clear that there would be no reception following the burial. Their uncle had left them half of his large crypt, so those details were all taken care of. But Dyllis did have one very peculiar demand. It seemed that the sisters had both lived with a morbid fear of not being able to get in touch with one another. And so it was that the telephone company installed a phone in the crypt. This odd request gave the townsfolk fodder for months' worth of gossip, but in all fairness, the neighbours did rally around the surviving twin. It soon became apparent, though, that she didn't want or need the attention, and so after a time, life went back to the way it had always been—except that Dyllis was now alone in the house their uncle had left to them and she paid two phone bills every month.

Around the August long weekend one year, Stella realized that Dyllis hadn't been in to pay her phone bill. That was so unusual that, during her lunch break, she made a point of talking to MacTier's librarian, who then realized that Dyllis hadn't made her regular visit there, either. With great trepidation, the two women decided that they needed to check on the remaining twin.

When there was no answer at the door, they turned the handle and pushed the door ajar. "Hello?" they called over and over again before deciding they'd have to do what no one had done since Phyllis died. They walked into the house.

There, on the floor, lay Dyllis's still, cold body. Her eyes were as big as saucers, her mouth was gaping open, and her arms were flung out from her sides. Next to her right hand lay the telephone, with its receiver off the hook.

Once again, the townsfolk gathered together. No one ever knew the cause of death. It seemed that her heart had simply stopped beating. One thing everyone did know was that Dyllis would want her body to be placed in the crypt beside her sister's.

And so preparations were made, and a handful of men took her coffin to the graveyard. One man pried open the latch on the family crypt and stepped inside the dark, dank enclosure. A second later, he ran screaming from the tomb.

You see, the telephone, the one that had been buried with Phyllis, was now off the hook.

OLD AND UGLY

There had been a decided swagger in Kaitlyn's step ever since she'd been accepted into the most prestigious sorority on campus. It had taken six months of concentrated effort to work her way into the group, but it had been so worthwhile. These girls were the ultimate in cool, and now, by extension, so was she. She did hate having to give up all the extracurricular music programs she'd been involved in, but you could either be a band nerd or a member of the inner circle: no one could be both. Besides, it wasn't that big of a deal. There weren't any exciting band trips coming up, so she wasn't sacrificing the opportunity to go anywhere new or interesting, whereas being included with Emily and Lauren and the other classy girls made the mere act of going to school a thrill.

Best of all, this weekend they were all going glamping just outside of Halifax. Yes, that's right: glamping, meaning "glamorous camping." One of her sorority sisters knew a fabulous campground. She'd been there before and she had all the equipment. Better still, the girl's father was going to lend them his luxurious SUV for the weekend, so they'd even be arriving in style. Apparently, the tent had a shiny crystal chandelier and the bedding was linen. Even the dishes were fine china. Kaitlyn could hardly wait. No more band billets for this princess! She was sophisticated now. She sighed with happiness. Everything about her new life warmed Kaitlyn's smug little heart.

Today she was meeting all her new friends to plan the details for the trip ahead. As she walked to the coffee shop where they regularly hung out, she felt as though she was walking on air. As a matter of fact, her head was so far in the clouds as she hurried toward the café that she didn't see the elderly woman walking toward her until they bumped into one another—hard.

Kaitlyn could feel that she'd knocked the woman off balance. She reached out to steady her, but then she remembered her new status.

"Watch where you're going, you old crone!" Kaitlyn yelled with a decidedly superior tone in her voice.

"Ah, my precious," the woman replied, poking a gnarled finger in the girl's face. "You are more right than you know. I am old and wrinkled, but you are weak and shallow. One day, you will be old and wrinkled too. That day will come sooner than you think, missy, you mark my words."

"I'll mark nothing of yours!" Kaitlyn gritted her teeth and hurried away to the security of her new friends in their coffee shop hangout. She'd like to tell them about the altercation she'd just had and the cool way she'd handled it, but at the last minute decided not to. She didn't want anything even remotely negative to come between her and her bright, promising future of popularity.

The café was warm and welcoming with the aroma of coffee and freshly baked pastries. Kaitlyn's friends were gathered around their usual table near the fireplace and welcomed her into the fold. An hour later, with all their plans in place, the girls hugged goodbye and went their separate ways.

Kaitlyn was so excited that it was after midnight before she fell asleep. Despite that, she sprang from bed in the morning just as she had been doing every morning since becoming one of the campus queens. She pulled the curtains back and looked out at an absolutely beautiful day, perfect for glamping. Turning back, she caught a glimpse of her reflection in her bedroom mirror. Then she screamed at the top of her lungs. The ugly, wrinkled face of an old crone stared back at her from the mirror.

THE LOAN SHARK

Mary Beth and Gary had just moved to an isolated town in rural Quebec to start new jobs. The move had been expensive, and the first week in their new home, they found themselves short of money. There was no point in going to the bank for a loan, because they had nothing to offer as collateral. They had no choice but to seek out a loan shark.

A man Gary knew at work told him who the local loan shark was, but warned Gary against his plan.

"Don't go to Slade for money," the man advised. "He'll bleed you dry."

"Thanks for the advice, but I wasn't born yesterday," Gary replied. "Sure, the interest will be horrendous, but what else are we supposed to do?"

The very next day, Gary went to meet with the man named Slade, whose office was above the general store.

"Is Slade upstairs?" he asked the woman behind the cash register.

The woman had met Gary and Mary Beth in the store a couple of times and had taken a liking to the young couple. "Don't go to Slade," she said, as she wrung her hands nervously. "You and Mary Beth have your whole lives ahead of you."

Gary shrugged. "It's not as if I have a choice."

With a look of great pain, the woman sighed heavily and ushered Gary to a narrow staircase tucked between shelves of duct tape and shoelaces.

"Be careful," she whispered. "He'll bleed you dry!"

Gary looked up at the steep set of dark stairs. He knew that once he took that first step, there was no way out. Every fibre in his body screamed at him to stop, turn around, and run away, but he ignored his body's signals and lifted one foot after another up the creaking staircase.

At the top of the stairs was a closed door. Gary knocked tentatively, so tentatively that even he could barely hear his knuckles rapping on the wooden door. He took a deep breath and knocked again, more forcefully this time.

"Do come in," a man's deep, cultured-sounding voice called out from the other side of the door.

Gary was taken aback. He had not been expecting such a polite-sounding invitation from a loan shark, a person with such a fearful reputation. Somewhat relieved, he opened the door and walked in.

What he saw was nothing like what he'd been expecting. The room was tastefully and expensively furnished. Carved wood panelling covered every wall, and the drapes pulled shut across the windows were thick and luxurious. There were even long, tapered candles placed around the room, all of them lit. What a jarring contrast to the nervous woman in the general store downstairs.

Slade sat in an enormous chair, wearing an expensive suit and sipping a beverage.

"Are you Gary?" Slade asked.

Gary nodded nervously and then added, "I need to do business with you."

Slade smiled and directed him to sit in a beautifully upholstered chair.

"Please sit down," he said, "and I will explain the terms of the contract."

Afterward, Gary took a minute to think over the details that Slade had just given him. He was nervous and desperate for the money, but he summoned his courage and said, "It's peculiar that you're not telling me what you want for collateral."

A look of impatience crossed Slade's face. "You're not dealing with a bank here, Gary. I work within my own terms. Essentially, I am only saying that if you cannot pay me on time, then I am free to take something from you. Something of my choice."

"Have you always done business this way?" Gary asked.

"That is none of your concern," came the loan shark's reply. "Let's just say that things are not the way they used to be. I've had to change with the times."

Gary hesitated for a second, but he and Mary Beth badly needed the money, so there was really no decision to make. Besides, he was confident that he could keep up the weekly payments, so the collateral would never become an issue.

"I agree, then," Gary said as he held out his hand. "I thank you for lending us the money."

For the first few weeks, everything went well. Gary dropped off his weekly payments at the general store, and he and Mary Beth went about their lives. But then he had to take a couple of days off work because of a toothache. Between the lost wages and the dentist's bill, there was just no money left to drop off at the general store.

Mary Beth was frantic. "The woman at the bakery says we should never have gone to Slade. She said he'll bleed you dry!"

"Don't worry," Gary assured her. "I've met him. Slade is not a thug. Besides, he can't take what we don't have."

Despite his brave words to Mary Beth, Gary was nervous as he trudged through the cold, dark streets on his way to the general store.

The woman behind the counter would scarcely look at him when he walked through the door. She nodded her head toward the nondescript door that led to the staircase and Slade's office. Gary thought he might have heard her whisper under her breath, "He'll bleed you dry."

As frightened as he could ever remember being, Gary climbed the stairs and knocked on the door at the top. He was expecting to be greeted by a posse of thugs, but when he opened the door he was relieved to find Slade sitting in his chair as calm and well attired as before. What Slade wasn't, though, was the least bit sympathetic about Gary's plight.

"You knew my terms," Slade said. "You agreed to them."

Finally, Gary realized that he could do nothing except honour their contract.

"Very well," he said. "What do you want from me?"

The loan shark smiled and showed Gary to a comfortable-looking couch, saying, "Sit here. It will only take a moment."

And it did.

That evening, Gary made his way home praying that his income would be higher the following week. When Mary Beth opened the door of their small apartment and saw her husband, he was as pale as a sheet and cold sweat dripped from his face. She screamed as he collapsed into her arms.

"I'll never borrow money from Slade again," he gasped as he fell on the sofa in utter exhaustion. Then he pulled away his collar to reveal two small puncture holes in the side of his neck.

"He really is going to bleed me dry," Gary said just before Mary Beth fainted.

THE SWIMMER'S GHOST

Michelle and her thirteen-year-old daughter, Hannah, had been looking forward to their vacation at Argyle Beach on the south shore of Prince Edward Island. When they arrived at the resort, they settled into their cabin before going to the main lodge for dinner. Most of the guests had already eaten, so they had the place to themselves. Just as they were finishing dessert, a tall, muscular young man came into the dining room.

"Hello," he said to Michelle, extending his hand to shake hers. "I'm Edmund. My partner and I are guests here, too." The two made small talk for a few moments before Michelle turned toward Hannah. She had been intending to introduce her daughter, but it was clear by the girl's body language that Hannah had no interest in meeting this man.

"I'll be off now," Edmund said and strode out of the lodge.

"Why were you suddenly so shy?" Michelle asked.

"Sorry," Hannah said, "but I just didn't like that guy."

"You hadn't even met him."

"I know, but there was something about him that creeped me out."

Michelle wisely decided that the matter wasn't worth pursuing, especially not at the risk of ruining the first night of their holiday.

At breakfast the next morning, the resort's owner came over to greet Hannah and Michelle. "I'd like you to meet two other guests. They also arrived yesterday afternoon."

With that the owner indicated the man who'd introduced himself to Michelle at dinner and his partner, Cortina. Michelle smiled and nodded. Hannah ignored them and sat down to eat her breakfast.

But the resort owner was clearly not finished with his introductions. "Cortina and Edmund are both champion swimmers. They're staying here to enjoy the water and to work on their skills."

Hannah looked up briefly. The man was certainly handsome and healthy-looking, but there was still something about him that she didn't like. Cortina, his wife or girlfriend, also looked very fit and athletic, but to Hannah, the young woman didn't seem very happy.

Edmund smiled and said to Michelle, "We don't mean to be rude, but we're in a bit of a hurry. We want to get a good swim in before lunch."

The resort owner, who had lived in the area all his life, overheard the man's comment and warned the swimmers to be careful. "There are powerful tides and undertows out there," he told the two.

The young man merely smiled and put his arm around Cortina's shoulder as they walked outside into the sunshine. Edmund was laughing as though he didn't have a care in the world.

Hannah and Michelle finished their breakfast and then took a pot of tea out on the patio to enjoy the amazing views. A moment later, a movement on the nearby path caught their attention. It was Edmund stumbling toward them. He looked exhausted and very upset. Seconds later, he gasped and explained that his wife had been caught in an undertow and that he hadn't been able to rescue her.

Everyone at the resort came running. They immediately organized a search party. Michelle was about to volunteer to join the searchers when she realized that Hannah was uncharacteristically quiet. She looked at her daughter with concern. Neither of them had ever experienced anything like this, so no doubt the girl was feeling nervous.

"We'll stay here," Michelle offered. "In case Cortina finds her way back on her own."

Edmund nodded his head and turned toward the group that had assembled.

As the searchers left on their frantic, life-or-death mission, Michelle turned to her daughter and asked, "Are you all right?"

Hannah was silent for a moment and then said, "I'm confused. That man's wife, Cortina, she was right there. She was standing behind him. Her bathing suit was dripping wet and her hair was hanging in water-soaked ringlets. She was so wet, she was shimmering."

"What?"

"She was there, Mama. Didn't you see her? She was crying. She kept asking the man, 'How could you? How could you?'"

Michelle could hardly believe her ears. Hannah had always been such a sensible girl. She'd never been one to tell tall tales, and the two of them had been sitting together when the man came up the path—alone, as far as Michelle could see.

An hour later, the dejected search party returned to the resort. The owner went into the hotel to phone the police.

Hannah sensed that it would be better not to say anything about the shimmering image she could still see floating along the path: the ghost of the young woman who, in life, was a championship swimmer but who came to her death by drowning—accidental or otherwise. The next day, Edmund checked out of the hotel and was never heard from again.

As for Michelle and Hannah, they continued their stay at the resort, but neither of them as much as dipped a toe in the water. Over the years, Hannah often thought of the swimmer's ghost, but she never again spoke of her solitary supernatural encounter, nor did she ever have such an experience again.

THE VOICE

The year was 1889. The place was St. Martins Bay, New Brunswick. Young Jack Dyre had been hired to help crew a ship christened the *Union*. Dyre lived to be a sailor and looked forward to many adventures aboard the freighter but, like most of us, Jack worked to earn money, so when the opportunity to earn a little extra cash came up, he had jumped at the chance—especially since the assignment seemed to be an easy one. The *Union*'s captain and three other crew members all wanted to go ashore for the night, but someone needed to stay aboard the ship. Before long, the group of five had negotiated an arrangement and everyone was happy. Jack would stay on the ship and in return would have a little something extra in his pay packet.

After he'd said goodbye to his shipmates, Jack realized that there was really very little to do aboard the docked vessel, so he decided to go to bed early. Just before he bedded down, he made one final check of the ship. All was secure and quiet, so he fell into his bunk and was asleep in no time.

Not long afterward, though, he woke up with a start and sat straight up in bed. Jack was sure he had heard someone call out his name. Worse, the voice warned him to leave the ship immediately. Jack was terrified, but he also kept in mind that he was responsible for the ship: that meant he had to get out of bed and find the trespasser who had come onto the boat and spoken to him.

Despite a thorough search of the vessel he knew so well, Jack could not find anyone on board or anything unusual anywhere in the ship. Relieved, he returned to his bed, where, after tossing and turning for a few minutes, he fell back to sleep.

Just as he had drifted off into a deep sleep, the voice came again, "Jack Dyre, you must leave this ship now."

Even more terrified this time, Jack sat shivering in bed, the covers pulled up around him, trying to muster up the courage to do what he knew he had to do—check once again for an intruder aboard the ship.

Moments later, all the while talking out loud to himself, Dyre left the security of his bunk and once again inspected the ship, this time more carefully. This second search netted no more of an answer as to the origin of the strange message than the first one had. Badly confused and frightened, he returned to his bed, even though he knew falling asleep again would be impossible.

As he lay awake, pleading silently and futilely for morning to come quickly, he heard the voice again. "Jack Dyre, you must leave this ship now."

By daybreak, Dyre had had enough of staying alone aboard a spooky ship with voices that seemed to come from nowhere and everywhere bearing scary messages. He packed his belongings and was ready to leave the ship as soon as his captain returned. The frightened man had no idea what or who could have spoken to him during the night. He just knew for certain that he would never set sail on that vessel again.

Although the *Union*'s captain tried very hard to change his sailor's mind, Jack Dyre left, and the captain knew that a replacement for him would have to be found before they could set out again. There were dozens of other young men on the docks who wanted adventure, so he had no trouble hiring someone. The *Union*, with her core of senior crew and one new man, sailed out of the port by noon.

The captain could tell right away that this trip was not going to be a good one. There was almost no wind, and any progress the ship did make was merely caused by the tide. Once they were well out into St. Martins Bay, the wind died down completely. The *Union* and dozens of other ships were completely becalmed.

As experienced sailors, those stranded on the still waters knew there was nothing they could do except swab the decks and shine the brass on their ships while they waited for the wind to pick up.

For the *Union*, however, that time never did come. As she rested on the water's calm surface, the ship inexplicably overturned. The captain and one crew member were rescued. The man who had taken Jack Dyre's place was among the three whose bodies were never recovered.

And so, it would seem that heeding the phantom voice that had persisted in warning him throughout the previous night had saved Jack Dyre's life.

FATAL ERROR

Like everyone else his age, Lex had originally moved to Tofino on Vancouver Island for the surfing, and he had easily fallen in with a terrific group of friends. They had bonded pretty much instantly by challenging and supporting one another on the waves.

But when the others wanted to drive down to a carnival that had set up shop in a nearby town, Lex knew he'd have to come up with an excuse not to join them. At the same time, though, he also had to protect his reputation as being fearless.

"You guys go ahead. I need to get my gear in shape," he told them.

The truth was that not only was his gear in excellent shape, but Lex also had a seriously healthy dislike of carnivals. One summer, he'd worked security for a transportation company that helped to haul the mechanical rides around the country. That's when he'd learned once and for all that many of those carnies weren't exactly advertisements for sober living, and he wasn't about to trust his life to a machine that some hungover dude had put together.

Instead, he'd just stay home and wander around Main Street, maybe getting a coffee and a sandwich somewhere. And that was exactly what Lex was doing when a woman approached him.

"Can I help you?" he asked with an irritated tone in his voice. She was, after all, standing no more than a metre away and staring at him.

"My friend," she said in a low voice, "you need your fortune told. May I sit down?"

"Or, you could just go away and let me enjoy my lunch," he replied.

The woman sat down on the chair next to him and ran the bony fingers of her right hand down his arm. He looked at her more closely and decided she must have been the oldest person he had ever seen.

"I am Sophia," she whispered and then waited for Lex to introduce himself. When he didn't, she shrugged and expelled a cloud of foul breath. "No matter. Your name is not important, but my message to you is, and it's this: you will make a fatal error in judgement tomorrow—at exactly 1:30 A M."

Lex bolted from the coffee shop. The woman's words echoed in his head like a chant. He ran to the dock and looked out over the water. The waves always calmed his mind. *Slow down,* he told himself. *You're okay. That didn't really happen. Must've been extra-strong coffee.*

He had just managed to lower his pulse rate when he heard someone calling his name. *It can't be the old lady. I didn't tell her my name,* he thought. A second later, he heard it again, "Lex! What's wrong with you? Can't you hear me?"

The young man slouched in relief. Someone really had been calling his name; it was his friend Maya. He'd forgotten that she hadn't gone to the carnival with the others.

"Hi, Maya. I'm glad to see you," he said.

"The pleasure's all mine," she teased. "Want to hang out?"

Lex nodded. Maya took his arm and noticed that his muscles were taut. It was clear that something was troubling her friend.

"What's up?" she asked.

Lex replied by shaking his head. He was nowhere near ready to explain what had just happened to him. They strolled together in silence, Maya wondering what was troubling her friend and Lex replaying in his head the strange woman's threatening words.

A fatal error in judgement. What the heck did she mean by that? And who was she, anyway?

Finally, Maya stopped walking and turned to Lex. "What's wrong?" she asked quietly.

"Want to go to the pub?" Lex asked, avoiding her question.

"I don't want to see you have anything to drink in the state you're in," she replied.

"Well, then, don't come with me," he said and pulled away from her.

Inside the pub, the rumble of conversation and the music pulsed loudly, and soon Lex's world had lost its edginess. The strange woman in the coffee shop with her dire warning was disappearing from his mind. She had never existed, he told himself—just before she hurled herself back into his consciousness and swirled around menacingly.

The next thing he knew, people were pressing their faces close to him—too close. He moved his head to the side. They were all leaning over him, their faces pulsing, first closer, then farther away. He closed his eyes and welcomed the utter blackness. When he came to again, he was on the floor of a strange room. There was an unmade bed. *Someone must have brought me here. How humiliating,* he thought. Even worse, he'd obviously fallen out of the bed like a little kid. The whole thing was childish, really. *Put to bed like a baby.*

He propped himself up on his elbow. The room spun madly around his head, but he managed to spot a clock on a nightstand. Hah! It was 2:15 AM. He hadn't made a fatal error at 1:30 like that stupid old woman had said he would. He pulled himself up onto the bed and, with a great force of will, stood up. *Only a loser wakes up in some stranger's place,* he thought. He would get home tonight if it killed him. He opened the door and staggered down the corridor toward an exit sign.

Much to his surprise, his car was just outside the door. He fished in his jacket pocket and found the keys. It took forever to get the key into the ignition. Cursing his shaking hands, he aimed the small piece of metal time and time again until finally he felt the key slide into the slot. The radio came on—too loud— but anything was too loud right now.

He whimpered from the exertion of trying to keep his world in focus. He wrestled the gear selector into drive and noticed the small numbers on the dashboard clock: 2:25 am, and he was still alive.

"Stupid old bag!" he screamed into the empty car. He pressed his foot down on the accelerator pedal—at least he thought he did. *Press harder, you dumb dork.*

—

When they found his body twisted in his mangled car, the radio was still playing.

"Don't forget folks, tonight's the night we go back to standard time. If you didn't fix them at 2:00, now's the time to turn your clocks back an hour."

EVIL

In the summer of 1989, Sara and Paul were both more than ready for their holiday in Ontario's Haliburton Highlands. They'd planned to load up the car as soon as they got home from work on Friday so they'd be ready to leave the city first thing Saturday morning. But once they were all packed and ready to go, Paul's impatience got the better of him.

"Come on, let's not wait until tomorrow morning. Let's go now," he urged Sara, who was generally the more sensible of the two. "That way we can wake up in the woods tomorrow morning."

"But that means driving at night, and we don't even know exactly where we're going," Sara countered.

"Ah, but we do," Paul announced triumphantly as he took a piece of paper from his jacket pocket. "The guy who owns the place sent me directions to get there. It looks easy."

Sara looked at the piece of paper Paul had in his hand and laughed. "It looks like a kid wrote this with a red pencil crayon."

"Maybe so, but these are some pretty detailed directions, and look at the last line—he's even set up a big sign at the edge of the laneway into the cabin. It has our names on it so we'll know exactly where to turn."

144

"That is pretty sweet," Sara admitted. She hated to crush her husband's enthusiasm. "Then I guess we're heading off right now."

As they got into the car, Paul handed the directions to Sara. "The guy's handwriting is pretty funny, eh?" he said.

"I hope the cabin's neater than his writing," she replied.

The pair chuckled. Sara opened a bag of muffins and the thermos of tea she'd packed for the trip. Just over an hour later, they turned off the main highway and began to watch for their names on a sign. Sara spotted it first and burst into a fit of giggles. There, at the side of the road, was a piece of plywood with "Sara & Paul" scrawled across it.

Paul guffawed when he saw the sign. "It's even colour-coded red like his directions were! I'll bet the cabin's painted red too."

"Wait a minute. That sign's pretty creepy," Sara replied. "Look how the paint has run. It looks like our names are bleeding."

"You're too sensitive. He's just a sloppy guy."

Paul steered the car toward the sign and then drove slowly along a gravel path until they came to a grove of trees blocking the way. The sun had set, and the trees blocked any light that might have been left in the sky. The couple looked ahead and to either side, but there was no sign of a cabin, red or otherwise, anywhere to be seen.

"Are we trapped?" Sara asked.

"No," Paul assured her. "I could always back out of here, but it's pretty tight and I'd rather not."

"Plus, that doesn't get us to the cabin, which is the whole point of the endeavour."

"Let's get out and look around," Paul suggested.

Sara had no sooner stepped out of the car when she spotted a slash of red in the woods. "I'll bet that's the cabin!"

"Seriously?"

"It *does* look quaint," she said, trying to sound brave and optimistic.

"The owner wasn't kidding when he said the place was secluded. No one could ever find us here."

A quick chill ran down Sara's back.

They made their way as best they could through the brush and maze of trees to the red wooden building Sara had spotted.

"The guy said the key would be under the mat, and here it is," Paul said, picking up an ancient skeleton key. "The thing must be a hundred years old."

"Oh great, that means the cabin's that old too."

Paul inserted the key in the slot, but the lock wouldn't budge.

"Let me try it," said Sara, but she didn't have any luck either.

"This'll work," Paul said as he pushed the door open with his shoulder.

As they entered the dark cabin, a strange odour wafted around them. Paul shot a quizzical glance at Sara, who tried unsuccessfully to convince Paul and herself that the smell was from some sort of unusual cleaning product.

When they closed the cabin door, the stench grew worse. This was more than just an unpleasant smell: it seemed to bring heat with it, stifling heat, the kind that nearly takes your breath away.

Sara opened the window. Paul took off his shirt.

"Something's very wrong in here," Sara commented quietly, and then, under her breath added, "Only evil could bring this kind of sour-smelling heat."

Paul laughed nervously, trying not to reveal his concern.

"I think we should leave," Sara added.

"Then we've wasted the trip," Paul said, trying to smile. "Look, the inside's not so bad. It's cozy, and besides, I'm exhausted. Let's see if the bed's comfortable."

He lay down on the bed and patted the sheet next to him, but Sara shook her head and perched tentatively on a straight-backed chair, the only other piece of furniture in the room. She looked down at the old wooden floor so Paul wouldn't see that she was choking back tears. When she looked up again, Paul was fast asleep.

If only it wasn't so dark, she thought. When her eyes had adjusted to the lack of light, a small movement in the corner of the room attracted her attention. It was a shadow. She stared as the shape grew thicker, until it became a swirling mass of putrid black energy. At its centre was a pair of red eyes.

"Paul! We need to get out of here! Now!" Sara screamed.

Paul bolted upright. His eyes flew open and his jaw dropped when he saw the apparition and its terrifying eyes.

"This place is haunted!" Sarah yelled.

They ran from the cabin to the safety of their car. Only when they had the doors locked and had reversed out to the road did either of them speak again.

"It was straight-out evil in there," Sara said.

Paul stared into the night and shook his head.

"You don't agree?" she prompted. "If that wasn't pure evil, then what would you call it?"

"I wouldn't," he said slowly, his voice shaking. "I wouldn't call it anything, for fear it would answer."

THE WOLVES' WATERING HOLE

Once there was a wealthy farmer named Harold who lived and farmed in rural Saskatchewan. Harold's sister, Maeve, lived in a nearby city with her son, Lucas. It seemed that Lucas was a high-spirited young man, and his mother thought it would be best if he went to live with his uncle on the farm. Harold wasn't overly warm to his sister's idea, but he loved her, and so he relented.

Sadly, Harold regretted his decision from the day Lucas arrived, bringing his knife collection with him. The boy was rude to Harold's wife and mean to his children. The worst thing, though, was the wild stories he told that not only scared the children but also put grandiose ideas into their heads.

One evening at dinnertime, Lucas began spinning a yarn, saying that he'd been out walking that afternoon and had come upon a lovely little stream of fresh, cool water.

"You must know it," he said to everyone gathered around the dinner table. "It's just at the edge of your farm, over by the woods."

The farmer's children shook their heads. They weren't allowed to go that far away from the farmhouse.

Lucas continued by telling the family that he had stopped for a long drink of water from the stream. "I noticed that it had a most peculiar, coppery taste, like blood," he said. "So when I came back home, I mentioned this to your farmhand, Jerome."

For a moment, Lucas stopped talking, put his fork down, and slapped his hands down on the table. Laughing mirthlessly, he continued, "What a hillbilly that Jerome is! He turned as pale as milk! He told me that I had just drunk from the wolves' watering hole. Then came the best part: he said that anyone who drinks that water becomes a werewolf."

The youngsters sitting at the table shivered with delighted fear. In their young imaginations, the prospect of transforming into a werewolf was immensely entertaining. Their father, however, scowled in disapproval.

"Jerome is a superstitious fool," he snapped. "Don't be telling my children his stories. Besides, wolves are no laughing matter to someone like me who owns livestock."

Lucas knew he'd found another way to torment his uncle, so that night before the little ones went to sleep, he whispered to each of them, "I could become a wild beast any moment now."

The weeks went by, and Harold's misery intensified. One day, Lucas took one of his little cousins to see a circus that was visiting town, and he smuggled the child into the freak show. The little boy didn't sleep for days after that. Another day, Lucas was caught kissing the preacher's daughter, who had come to the farm hoping to collect a contribution for the church. Worse still, the young man showed no respect for Harold's authority, which caused the farmer constant aggravation and embarrassment. To relieve his stress, Harold complained about the situation to anyone who would listen.

"He's a terrible boy," Harold told his neighbour. "He's causing great disruption in my house."

"I never should have agreed to let him live in my house," he said to the town's mayor. "He'll be the ruination of my reputation."

"I've never heard such wild lies in all my life," Harold confided to the bank manager. "You can't believe a word that comes out of his mouth."

Soon, Harold also had a new problem. The wolves in the countryside had become much more aggressive and were slaughtering the lambs from his flock. One day, Lucas overheard his uncle complaining about losing valuable livestock.

"Perhaps," Lucas suggested, smiling, "the wolves are angry that I drank from their stream."

"This is nothing to smile about!" Harold shouted, and stormed out of the room, determined to get in touch with his sister the following week to tell her Lucas simply had to go back to live with her in the city. For now, though, his most pressing problem was to find a way to preserve his lambs.

And so it was that on the first night of the next full moon, Harold loaded his rifle and hid away in the loft of the barn. From his vantage point, with the bright clear light of the moon shining through the slats in the barn's wood frame, he had a fine view of all the animals in their pens and would be able to see any predators well in advance of their arrival.

"Now, let the beast show itself," he muttered as he settled down to watch. But hours passed and nothing happened. Eventually, Harold drifted off to sleep.

He woke to the tortured cry of a lamb.

"Who's there?" Harold yelled as he grabbed his rifle and scanned the animals' pens. What he saw nearly shocked him into dropping his rifle.

It was a wolf, but not the ordinary kind of wolf that he had been expecting. It was the largest beast he had ever seen. The creature stood as many hands high as a small horse. Its head was massive and thick. But none of this disturbed Harold as much as the sight of the monster clutching a large wounded lamb in its two front paws, while balancing perfectly well on its hindquarters.

"Saints above, save me," Harold pleaded under his breath as he raised his rifle and peered through the sight. Even though he had whispered, the wolf seemed to have heard him and looked up to the loft with bright-red eyes. Then its mouth opened and, for a moment, Harold could have sworn that the beast smiled a mocking sort of smile at him.

Harold's heart beat hard and fast in his chest. He held his rifle as steady as he could and squeezed the trigger.

The animal dropped the lamb and howled. Blood oozed out, staining its matted fur as it writhed in pain. As the stain grew larger, the wolf appeared to grow smaller and smaller. Finally, when the beast fell to the ground, it no longer dwarfed the slain lamb that lay beside it.

How can it be? Harold wondered. He could no longer believe his own two eyes. Then he doubted his ears as the wolf let out a final anguished cry that sounded more like a human lament. Finally, with a smaller sound, strangely like distant laughter, the creature perished.

Shaking with fear, Harold climbed down from the loft. He needed to assure himself that the unnatural beast was truly dead. Even from that distance he could see that it had stopped breathing. He leaned against a hay bale as he recovered his composure.

Soon Harold's fear had subsided and his confidence grew. *I'll mount the head*, he thought, *and display it in the house.* But as he drew closer to the crumpled body lying in the corner of the barn, he realized that it could never happen.

There was no wolf there: only the naked mud-and-blood-streaked corpse of his nephew.

HOT PINK

Susan and Emily had been best friends since the eighth grade. It was no surprise then, that after high school graduation, they took jobs together at a resort in Ontario's Thousand Islands. They even shared a small room in an auxiliary staff building.

Susan had missed taking grade-twelve biology, so she was doing the course online during the summer. She liked to study in the evenings as soon as she was off work.

One evening, after a particularly difficult day, Emily was exhausted and asked her friend if she could study somewhere else. Susan was sympathetic, especially as she liked to listen to music while she studied, so she readily agreed to leave the room. She gathered up her books and papers and made her way to the staff lounge in the next building. She had been reviewing her notes for less than an hour when a group of fellow employees came to talk to her. They told her she looked like she needed a break and that they were on their way into town. "Why don't you join us?" one suggested.

Susan hesitated for only a moment before she decided that hanging out with her new friends would be much more fun than memorizing the various parts of insects' bodies.

"I just need to go to my room to get my wallet and a sweater," she told the others. "Wait here for me, and I'll be right back."

Susan ran into the dorm building and then went quietly along the hall until she came to the room she shared with Emily. Ever so slowly and quietly, she put her key into the lock and opened the door. Emily was not known for her pleasant disposition when she first woke up, so Susan really didn't want to disturb her.

Fortunately, she knew their little room like the back of her hand, which meant she wouldn't have to turn on the light. Susan stepped quietly into the darkness and gently closed the door behind her. She took a few steps into the room with her hands held out cautiously. When her fingers touched the little desk where she did most of her studying, she stopped. She set her books on the desktop and then, very slowly and quietly, pulled open the top drawer. A few seconds later, she felt the familiar worn leather of her wallet. She picked it up, closed the drawer, and inched across the room toward the one tiny closet the two girls shared. Her roommate had left it open, which made it easier to quietly reach inside and grope around until she felt the nubby woollen sleeve of her cardigan. As quietly as she could, she slipped the sweater from its hanger and wrapped it around her shoulders. Then, on a whim, she ran her hand along a shelf in the closet and picked up her roommate's new hot-pink lipstick that she'd bought to match her favourite nail polish. Tucking the lipstick in her pocket to apply as soon as she had more light, Susan left the room, closing the door as gently as she had opened it.

A few moments later, she rejoined her friends, who had been waiting patiently outside the staff lounge. Then they all headed into town, where they had a fine time wandering along the main street before stopping for coffee.

Several hours later, they got back to the resort. Susan said good night to the others as they went into the main staff building before walking to the auxiliary building where she and Emily had their room.

As she rounded the corner, Susan was met by a most disturbing scene. Police cruisers were parked in front of the building, with lights flashing in an eerie rhythm. Crime-scene barricades stood on the lawn, which swarmed with uniformed cops and somber-looking detectives.

"What happened here?" Susan asked person after person. No one would give her an answer. "Is someone hurt? Who is it?" she pleaded, feeling panic rise in her throat. "I have to know if my friend's all right!"

"There will be a statement issued in the morning," was all anyone would say. But Susan couldn't wait until then to find out if Emily was okay. She darted into the building and up the staircase, ignoring the barricades and ducking under the lines of yellow crime-scene tape. She dodged every person who tried to stop her and ran until she reached the hall outside her door. She was horrified to see the tiny room crowded with investigators.

"Who let this girl in?" barked a red-faced detective who appeared to be in charge.

"Please," Susan gasped, "this is my room! I need to find my friend Emily."

The detective softened a little and walked over to Susan's side.

"I'm sorry," he said. "We'll need to talk to you, miss. Your friend was attacked. We think it happened about seven thirty."

Susan felt faint.

"That's impossible!" she said. "I stopped back here about seven thirty. Everything was fine."

"You were here, this evening?" asked the detective.

"Yes, for a minute. To get a sweater and my wallet." She didn't add that she'd also taken her friend's new pink lipstick.

"Well, then," the detective said, "perhaps you can help us make sense of something."

He led her into the room then, being careful to shield her eyes from the grisly scene being photographed and investigated. He directed her into the bathroom and flipped on the light switch.

"Do you have any idea what this means?" the detective asked the student. He pointed to the mirror.

Susan looked up and felt her knees weaken. Written on the glass, in dried streaks of hot-pink nail polish, was a message. A message that had clearly been left for her. It read: *Aren't you glad you didn't turn on the lights?*

AN APPARITION STILL VISITS

Conception Bay on Newfoundland's southeast coast is a place of breathtaking beauty, and the town of Clarke's Beach lies at the mouth of the North River in that bay. Long ago, a train ran through the little towns that once dotted the river's path with trestle bridges built to carry the trains over valleys. Some of those old bridges, still covered in railway tracks, were left to stand for many years after the trains had chugged off into history. And it was toward one of those trestles that three teen-aged friends were walking on a summer's day.

The friends, Louise, Joyce, and Monica, loved to talk to one another in privacy, so the isolated spot was one of their favourite areas. And this was a perfect day for a walk. The sun shone brightly, and the air blowing in from the North Atlantic was crisp and clean.

They walked along happily, enjoying the views and one another's company. Soon they came to the deteriorating old trestle bridge, and Monica suddenly stopped in her tracks.

"What's that?" she asked, pointing toward the bridge.

"The bridge, silly," Joyce replied jokingly as she gave her friend a nudge with her elbow to move her along.

But Monica wasn't moving, and neither was Louise. Slowly, Joyce looked in the direction the two were staring. At first she couldn't see anything unusual, but then she noticed a patch of dark mist off in the distance at the other end of the bridge. The cloud undulated and intensified.

"Let's go home!" Joyce whispered, her voice quivering.

"Where's your sense of adventure?" Louise asked, slowly walking toward the shape.

"Come on. We can hold hands. I want to see the mist up close. I've never seen anything like this," Monica said.

"You're too curious for your own good," Joyce told her firmly, but Monica had already grasped her friends' hands for courage, so the three walked slowly toward the image. Then they stopped. What they were looking at was no longer a misty shape but the distinct image of a young woman about their own age, wearing a bathing suit. She didn't seem to have noticed the three approaching but just stood, drying her long, blonde hair with a towel.

The trio took a step closer. This seemed to catch the figure's attention. Slowly the apparition turned her head and stared at them—with empty eye sockets.

The girls ran screaming from the bridge and the phantom standing on it. By the time the three reached the safety of town, they were crying and gasping for air. Several people heard the ruckus and came out of their houses to see what was wrong. It was a long while before Joyce, Louise, or Monica could speak, and then another while before they were able to speak coherently enough to be understood.

Once they were calm enough, they described the dark mist that had morphed into a young woman in a bathing suit drying her hair. A few of the people who had gathered around them began to nod their heads.

"We thought her spirit had moved on by now," a man said quietly.

"She hasn't been seen for years," another person said.

"What are you people talking about?" Joyce shouted in frustration.

The man who had spoken first began to explain. "The vision you saw was the ghost of a young woman. Legend has it that she and her lover had slipped away for a secret midnight swim. Neither of them was ever seen again."

The man took a deep breath before continuing. "All that remains is her spectre, and even that is seen less and less often these days. They say the empty eye sockets are the most haunting part of any sighting."

Tears of fear mixed with a healthy dose of compassion for the poor dead girl ran down the three girls' cheeks. They decided then and there to find another place to walk and talk, because that was not an encounter they ever wanted to experience again.

STORIES
BY LANTERN
LICHT

THE LAST SEASON

Every year when the "boys of summer" hit the Kamloops area, the whole place came alive. Whenever there was a homestand, many girls and young women spruced themselves up to make an impression on the handsome young athletes who played on the out-of-town teams. Of course, as soon as the girls were all gussied up, all the local boys, not just the ones on the baseball team, took notice—no visitors were going to steal *their* girls—so the hometown lads would show the local lasses considerably more attention. It seemed that once baseball season arrived, everyone and everything perked up—even the economy.

Yes, sir, baseball just made people happy, and that was a good thing, because in the 1930s, there really wasn't much to be happy about. You can take it from me—after all, I was the local team's manager for its entire existence. But there's more to the story, much more. And it's a sad and puzzling story, actually.

Bert Barrow—he was our star player. That boy had a golden arm, I tell you. How he could pitch! Mind you, Bert was no spring chicken. He had been a pilot in the Great War. Just the fact that we had our own "flyboy" was enough to do us proud, but then when Bert turned out to be the best pitcher in the league, and a nice guy on top of it all—well, the whole town just came to love him.

Now you might not believe me, but we won the pennant in our starting season—took the final series in four straight. At the end of the last inning, everyone was whooping and hollering and celebrating so much that no one noticed Bert wasn't around. Well, that guy, he was such a character. Instead of sticking around with the others, he ran over to the airstrip, and a few minutes later, darned if he didn't fly over the ball diamond, swoop real low, and throw a bunch of candies down to the kids. All the while, you could hear him yelling, "Yee haw!" Yup, he was a popular fellow, that Bert.

Later that fall, Bert flew north to go hunting. He never came back. We searched as best we were able, but a ground search wasn't good enough. We needed to hire a pilot and a plane to look for him properly, but we just didn't have that kind of money—things were hard during the Depression. The only person in town who did have the money was the ball club's owner, and he was just too cheap. It was a sad, sad thing, I'll tell you.

The team took Bert's disappearance hard—not just the team, actually: everyone around town did. The next season, we didn't even make it to the playoffs—nor the next, nor the next, nor the next. By then, no one was bothering to come out to watch the games, so the owner wasn't making any money. It seemed our hearts had disappeared with Bert.

The winter after that fifth season, the owner sold the club for a pittance. All of us, the players and me, we thought our playing days were over. But this new owner, well, he was an interesting guy. The first thing he did come spring was rent a plane and hire a pilot. It took more than a week, but finally the pilot spotted the wreckage of Bert's plane. No one knows why, but Bert had crashed into some pretty dense bush.

Well, once we had the coordinates, a bunch of guys went in and found Bert—what was left of him, that is. He was still strapped into the pilot's seat. It looked like he'd died on impact. His body had just sat there in that cockpit, rotting, for nearly five years. It was terrible. The only thing we could do was bring his remains home so we could finally give him a decent burial. People came from all around to attend the funeral and pay their respects to Bert.

At the season's home opener a few weeks later, we had a minute of silence. Once the game started, it was like we were on fire. We all but blew our opponents out of the ballpark. We won the game by a huge margin, and then the next game and the next and the next until we went on to win the pennant.

It was a glorious moment for all of us, but I think especially for the team's new owner. Some people believed that it was as if Bert Barrow's once-restless spirit was saying "thank you" to the man who had finally been responsible for finding his remains. Other ones, they said that Bert's spirit had been so angry about his body being left to rot that he'd put a curse on that first owner.

I sure do wish that I could tell you the team kept right on winning those baseball seasons, but I can't. Our chances were looking good for the 1939 season, but then the war came and lots of us never played baseball again. Not here on Earth anyway. Maybe there were some good innings thrown in the great beyond with Bert on the mound.

There's just one other point I should mention, I guess. The baseball club's first owner—the one who wouldn't even pay a dead man, his former star pitcher, the courtesy of funding a proper search—well, that man lived to be well over ninety years of age. But from the day we found Bert's body, it was as if that old owner was haunted—acted real peculiar from that day forward. He rarely left his house, and when he did, you could see him looking over his shoulder as though something scary was following him.

ROOM FOR ONE MORE

Never in all his life did Simon think that he'd be grateful for a nightmare. Especially not one he'd had over and over again. For as long as he could remember, his life had been the same misery. The terror, the lack of sleep, the anxiety, but what he really hated was that he'd wake up screaming like a little kid.

No, "grateful" hadn't even come close to how he felt about the recurring nightmare. It was always the same. He dreamed that he was inside a palace—a huge, luxurious, old palace. There were enormous chandeliers hanging from the ceiling, velvet draperies hanging from the windows, and thick rugs on the floor. Then he would hear a noise outside, as if horses' hooves were trotting along a gravel road. Simon would want to look outside, but as soon as he tried to move, he realized that he was tightly wrapped in tattered rags, like the mummy he had seen in a museum on a school field trip a decade or more ago. Despite the rags, he would always manage to make his way to the window, where he would see a team of black horses pulling a wooden wagon. When he looked more closely, he could see the horses' eyes, burning red, like embers of burning coal.

As the terrifying contraption moved closer to him, Simon could see that the wagon the horses were pulling was piled high with coffins. In his dream, he somehow knew that each coffin held a decaying corpse. He would always try to move away from the window so that he wouldn't have to look at the gruesome sight, but he never succeeded. And that would be when he saw the horses' driver—a veritable skeleton of a man, his eyes beady and his nose hawk-shaped. Seconds later, the horrible-looking man's thin lips would part, and he would look up and call out to Simon, "Room for one more!"

One summer, Simon simply couldn't take the stress of the nightmares any longer. He was constantly exhausted and couldn't concentrate. He started making mistakes at work. His boss had already reprimanded him once. His wife was fed up with being awakened in the middle of the night by her husband thrashing about and twisting the sheets around himself.

In short, the man's life was falling apart. He had to get away. Fortunately, his wife's uncle owned an old resort hotel on the outskirts of a small town in northern Quebec. Apparently, it had been quite the place in its day but had become run down over the years. The uncle needed help with some renovations, and Simon needed a quiet place to go, so the arrangement seemed like a match made in heaven.

As Simon drove north, he could feel the stress and anxiety falling away.

Once he found the old place, he realized that his wife's uncle had understated the situation—in a major way. The resort looked like a rundown old castle. Simon sucked up a deep breath and slowly made his way up the stairs to the once-grand entrance.

He opened the door and stepped into an enormous lobby. The floor was covered with worn carpeting, and tattered velvet drapes hung from the huge windows. The frames of what had once been grand chandeliers were suspended from the ceilings at various angles. Straight ahead of him was a bank of elevators that had, no doubt, been splendid in their day, with their polished brass doors adorned with intricate designs. He pictured uniformed operators back in the day when guests were too refined to push their own button for whatever floor they wanted.

Simon looked around. *This place is like an abandoned palace,* he thought.

And that's when Simon started to feel very uncomfortable. His skin crawled with goose bumps, and waves of nausea flooded through his body. His chest tightened, and his stomach clenched.

An elevator door slid open. "Good afternoon, sir. This way, please." That voice! It was so familiar. Was it his wife's uncle? No, he didn't think so. Simon's frantic mind wouldn't calm down enough to let him figure out how he knew that voice. He tried to get a breath, but he couldn't. His head was swimming. He was terrified.

But, of course, being Canadian, he didn't want to appear rude. Slowly, almost against his own will, he walked toward the elevator operator who had greeted him. He tried shaking his head to indicate "No," but his neck muscles would not cooperate: he was quite literally paralyzed with fear. He looked at the elevator operator. Could this be his nightmare come to life? No, that certainly wasn't the man in his dream. This was a respectable-looking man—except that he didn't seem solid. He was a shimmering mirage. Cold sweat ran down Simon's face.

Suddenly the elevator was crowded with people, all dressed in fancy, old-fashioned clothes. Simon gulped and finally croaked out a high-pitched "no, thank you" as he shuffled backward across the lobby toward the front door. An instant later, he turned to run, looking back only once to see the elevator operator one last time. He was a veritable skeleton of a man, his eyes beady and his nose hawk-shaped. This was the man from his nightmare.

Then the horrible-looking apparition parted its thin lips and called out to Simon, "Room for one more!"

Simon ran from the decrepit hotel and out into the fresh air and sunshine.

That's when he heard the screams, the ghostly wails of the long-dead elevator occupants meeting their deaths once again. He had almost been with them.

Simon bolted for his car and drove, with great caution, back home. As he drove, he pondered what had happened. He realized that his nightmares had been premonitions, warnings that had saved his life. He felt grateful now that he'd had them.

His wife greeted him with stony silence. When she finally did speak to him, it was clear that she wasn't in a mood to be sympathetic.

"My uncle phoned," she began. "He said you didn't show up

today. What's wrong with you, Simon? Are you ever going to get your life together, or are you going to let that silly nightmare ruin everything till the day you go to your grave?"

Simon looked at his wife. He'd put her through a lot, but now, finally, he was able to say with conviction, "No, that nightmare is history. Today is definitely the first day of the rest of my life."

WHERE IS MICHAEL?

Twelve-year-old Michael Norton was a happy little boy who lived with his family on a farm near Burtons Falls, Ontario. One morning after breakfast, the child headed out as usual to do his chores in the barn before it was time to get his school-bag and walk with his brother and sister to the road, where they would wait for the school bus. His mother watched him walk past one of the outbuildings before she went back to cleaning up the kitchen. After that, Michael waved to his aunt, who lived in a small house nearby, and said good morning to his father's farmhands.

When Michael still hadn't come back into the house to get his schoolbag, his mother began calling for him, while his brother and sister, who didn't want to miss the bus, waited impatiently. When Michael didn't respond to his mother's calls, his father headed out to look for the boy in the barn. The man found the milking stool near one of the cows and a bucket half-filled with milk. What he didn't find was any trace of Michael. Clearly, the boy had stopped in the middle of his work. Whatever could have taken him away so suddenly, his father wondered. He asked the farmhands if they knew where he was, but neither of them had seen him since they'd exchanged greetings an hour or so earlier.

Soon everyone on the farm was out scouring the buildings and fields in search of young Michael, while his father drove to the police station to report his son missing. An organized search party that included a specially trained police dog set out. The animal picked up Michael's scent almost immediately and excitedly followed a trail that led from the house to the barn and back out again before veering into the pasture. Then the dog stopped, sat down, and refused to move, despite his handler's urgings. It seemed that Michael's trail had stopped in the middle of an open field, in plain view of the house, the barn, and even the road.

This was too puzzling to be believed, so the police brought in another dog and the community organized a larger search party. The boy couldn't have just vanished—could he? As the search went on into its second and third day, it seemed as though that was exactly what had happened.

Then, on the third night, Michael's mother and father heard a familiar voice call "Mum!" They ran from room to room in the house, but there was no sign of their son, so they went outside. As they stood in the empty yard, they heard it again: "Mum!" But this time, the disembodied voice added, "Where are you?"

The Nortons called to their son, asking him where he was, but they received no answer. At least they knew he was somewhere on the property. They called in neighbours to help look and even hired a search plane to check old wells, gullies, and even a newly formed crack in the ground where he might have fallen. Hours later, they were all frustrated by their lack of success. Worse, dozens of people heard the boy's voice calling out to his mother.

Days went by, but Michael was not to be found, even though he could still be heard calling for his mother. By the second week after his disappearance, Michael's voice had grown fainter.

The hunt for the missing child went on for years, because although he disappeared physically, both his parents and hundreds of investigators had all heard Michael's voice—calling faintly from the same few square metres of ground.

One theory proposed was that Michael Norton had somehow fallen through the veil of time. That theory might sound far-fetched, but no more so than the indisputable fact that in 1935, a twelve-year-old boy named Michael Norton disappeared into thin air.

A SHADOW IN THE NIGHT

On a May long weekend back in the late 1990s, Peter and Kyle were hunkered down for the night in a cabin near Haines Junction in Yukon. Well, perhaps the moniker "cabin" is a bit of a stretch. No one could ever picture a family enjoying their summer vacation where these two men were staying, because their shelter for the weekend was nothing more than a small trailer, the kind that gets towed out to a construction site to be used as a temporary office, staff room, and general catchall. You see, Peter and Kyle were scientists, forced to spend the night in the spartan laboratory set up to monitor the area's ecology.

Their trip to the lake was an annual event that both men usually looked forward to, but this year a spring blizzard had hit late on Saturday afternoon, and now they were stranded. All they could think about was getting the next day's work done so they could shovel themselves out and head back to Dawson City. For now, though, they could only kill time until they were both tired enough to fall asleep.

As he always did, Peter had brought along Timber, his elderly, blue-eyed husky, and both he and Kyle were glad to have the dog with them. Her calm, affectionate nature meant she was always good company, even though she'd been snoozing under their worktable for most of the evening.

Kyle had already fallen asleep when Timber began to whine. Pete rubbed the dog's head, as he always did when the old girl was having one of her doggie nightmares. But a moment later, she was up on all fours, growling menacingly.

"It's okay, girl," Peter said quietly. "Just relax. You're all right."

But clearly Timber was not all right, and she most assuredly was not relaxed. Her ears were twitching, and she was pawing at the worn linoleum beneath her feet.

"Come on up here," Pete told the dog, patting the side of his bunk. Uncharacteristically, the dog didn't jump at the invitation.

"What's wrong with her?" Kyle asked sleepily.

"No idea. I've never seen her like this before."

Outside, the wind howled. Pellets of icy snow pinged against the cabin's windows.

"Must be the storm. It's pretty noisy. I actually thought I heard someone knocking on the door a few minutes ago."

But Kyle didn't hear his friend's comment. He was already snoring again.

Pete lifted Timber up onto the bed beside him. An unfamiliar growling reverberated in the dog's throat. From the top bunk, the sound of Kyle's snoring competed with the noise of the wind outside. With the warmth of his dog's body beside him, Pete drifted into an uneasy sleep—until something startled him awake again.

Sitting bolt upright, he looked around the darkened room. Nothing he could see had changed. The wind still pounded snow and ice against the trailer's metal frame. But now there was another noise, too. Was that what had woken him? Was someone knocking at the window? No, that wasn't possible. No one could have made their way through this blizzard. Maybe it was just a branch from a nearby tree banging against the glass.

Timber cowered against the far wall of the bed, whimpering. The fur on her neck was standing on end.

"It's okay, girl. It's only the wind," Pete said, trying to console the frightened animal. "It'll be morning soon, and then we'll be on our way home."

But there it was again, that knocking sound. *Just tree branches,* Pete told himself over and over again until he suddenly remembered that the trailer was parked in a clearing; there weren't any trees for at least thirty metres. Tree branches could not possibly be knocking against the window. His body went rigid. *So this is what it's like to be paralyzed with fear,* he thought. He took several deep breaths. *Lie down,* he told himself. *There's no danger.*

Pete obeyed his own instructions and lay down again, but no matter how much he tried, he couldn't make his eyelids close.

The knocking kept up. Were there shutters beside the window frames? Could those be banging? No. Someone was knocking on the door, and Pete knew that he couldn't ignore it. A person would freeze to death out there in that storm. *How can Kyle be sleeping through all of this,* he wondered resentfully.

Pulling on his jacket and boots first, Pete reached for the door, but before he could unlock the handle, a shadow filled the doorway. He jumped back in terror. Timber yelped and slid under the bed. Kyle slept on. The temperature in the room plummeted.

Pete pinched his wrist and rubbed his eyes. This wasn't a nightmare. Something was in the trailer with them because there, towering over him not a metre away, was an indistinct shadow floating just off the floor. Pete tried to cry out for help but couldn't make a sound. The shadow thickened and lengthened into the form of a man. For a moment, Pete was relieved. Perhaps this was just some traveller lost in the storm, but even as he thought that, Pete knew he was lying to himself; for one thing, he hadn't actually opened the door, so how had it gotten in? The entity stared at him with glowing red eyes. Its shape shifted and morphed until it was too dense to be a shadow. It had a face, shoulders, and arms. Then the apparition reached out a hand to the terrified man.

Timber whimpered pitifully.

Pete backed away. *Is this the Devil? I'm not going to find out by shaking his hand.*

Every fibre of Pete's body wanted to scream "Get out!" at the unnatural intruder, but he couldn't make a sound. Besides, what if it was a person? A person couldn't survive out in that storm. *But what if I'm right and it isn't a person?* Pete thought.

"For Kyle," the being whispered in a gravelly voice and extended its arm down toward the counter that held the men's testing equipment.

Pete looked down. Beside the microscope lay a small white card.

When he looked back up, the shadow had vanished.

Sweat dripped down Pete's face. His hands shook. He had to get a grip. What if that was a person? No one could survive more than a few seconds in that raging storm. What to do? Pete knew he couldn't go out after the man. That would mean his own sure death. He rubbed his sleeve against the frosted window. There was no sign of anyone or anything out there except snow and wind.

Timber leaped onto Pete's bed, pushing her trembling body against its far corner. The poor thing needed comfort; for that matter, so did Pete. He lay down beside the dog and sometime later fell asleep, his arm resting on her back.

By morning, the storm had blown through. Kyle was up early and anxious to finish their work.

"The sooner we can pile into that four-by-four and head south, the happier I'll be," Kyle said, but Pete was not listening.

What had happened last night? Had someone really been in the trailer, or had the whole thing been a dream?

A small puddle of icy water lay by the door. *The wind could've blown snow underneath*, Pete thought.

Forcing away his uncomfortable thoughts, Pete nodded and powered up the microscope. A small white card lay beside the instrument. He slid it off the table and into his backpack, pausing only long enough to read the one word written on it. It read JERRY.

By noon, their tasks completed, the men packed up, put on flannel shirts, parkas, fur-lined mitts, and mukluks. Kyle brushed off the truck and turned the key in the ignition. Much to his relief, the engine fired up right away. Pete packed up the testing equipment and stowed it in the back of the crew cab. Then, together, the men shovelled two tracks from the trailer to the access road. They knew that the drive to the highway would be tricky, but the truck was reliable and they were well familiar with winter driving conditions. With Kyle at the wheel, they were finally heading home.

For the first hour, neither man said a word. Kyle was concentrating on driving, while Pete's mind played the scenario of last night's strange encounter over and over again until he thought he would go insane if the infinite loop of thought didn't stop. Once they were safely on the highway, they both relaxed a little.

"Hard to believe it's May 19, eh?" Pete said as he stared at the white landscape surrounding them.

Kyle nodded, keeping his eyes on the road ahead. "Got any gum?"

"Might do. I'll check my backpack," Pete reached awkwardly to the floorboard behind his seat. Just as he jammed his hand into the pack to hunt for the gum, Kyle's phone rang. "Well, at least we know we're within cell coverage now," said Pete.

"Answer it for me, will you?" asked Kyle.

Pete nodded, swiped the phone face, and said, "Pete speaking."

"I thought this was Kyle's phone." Pete immediately recognized their boss's voice.

"Kyle's driving. What can we do for you, Todd?"

There was no reply. Pete wondered if the call had been dropped. They were probably still a long way from a cell tower. Finally the man said, "I need to speak to Kyle."

"There's no place to pull off the road here. If we stop for coffee, he can call you then."

With those arrangements made, Pete put down the phone and told Kyle the boss wanted him to call when they got to the next town.

Kyle nodded. "Guess I must've messed up on something. Not gonna stop for coffee. He can wait and chew me out once we're back at the office."

"That's your decision," Pete said as he stared out at the stark white world. He couldn't imagine his friend making a mistake at work. They'd been partners for years, and Pete knew that Kyle deserved his reputation as a perfectionist.

"Make with the gum, would you?"

"Oh, yeah, sorry." Pete reached into his backpack, but the first thing he pulled out of it wasn't a pack of gum. It was a small white card with the name JERRY printed in capital letters.

Pete's throat tightened. What happened last night wasn't a nightmare. It had been real. His hand shook as he slipped the card into his shirt pocket.

Kyle shifted in the driver's seat. "Do you have any gum or not? My mouth tastes like something died in it."

"Sorry," said Pete again, digging deeper in his backpack until he found a package of gum.

The men drove the rest of the way into the city in silence, Kyle concentrating on his driving while Pete agonized over his experience the night before and whether or not to say anything about the strange encounter—to anyone, ever.

Hours later, Kyle steered the truck into the nearly empty company parking lot. Both Pete's and Kyle's cars were buried in wet snow. A third one, almost free of snow, was parked close to the building's side door. They both recognized it as their boss's car.

"Something's hit the fan for sure, or Todd wouldn't be here waiting for us on a long weekend," Kyle said.

Pete's thoughts collided in his mind. His gut wrenched at the thought of what might be ahead. Should he try to explain about the shadowy figure and the card? But how? Kyle would think he'd lost his mind, and their boss certainly wouldn't take kindly to field scientists seeing strange apparitions in the middle of the night, especially not on company property.

"Good to see you two safely back in town. You can both take next weekend as a long weekend instead. Hopefully, the weather will be better then, too."

"Thanks, Todd, that's great," Kyle said. "But what did you want to talk to me about?"

"Your wife called me this morning. It seems her stepfather died last night. She wanted me to let you know that's she's fine and she'll call you from her mother's house this evening."

Kyle sighed in relief. "So I didn't mess up at work?"

"No, of course not. Your work's impeccable. Always has been."

"Good."

"So should we send flowers or something? From the company, you know?" Todd offered.

"No. Jerry was a miserable excuse for a human being. He had a heart as black as a noon-hour shadow."

Pete eased himself into a nearby chair. If he didn't know better, he could've sworn he saw a black shadow cross the wall by the door. But of course, that couldn't be.

Could it?

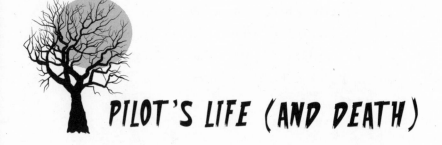

PILOT'S LIFE (AND DEATH)

Sasha climbed up the stairs to the small airplane and stepped inside the cabin. She was looking forward to a quiet flight home after a day full of high-pressure meetings. The private flight was a thank-you present from her boss—an extravagant demonstration of his appreciation for all the work she had done to land this especially big contract.

The pilot greeted her and helped her get settled, chatting the entire time. He told her about the weather in Medicine Hat, how many flights he'd made that day, that his daughter was only two years old and already talking (*No surprise there,* she thought), that his neighbour's dog barked constantly, and on and on until Sasha had a splitting headache. She mumbled a brief response, one that she hoped would not encourage his talkativeness, but the man seemed to be insensitive to subtle social cues. How ironic that her boss's consideration was going to make the short flight from Red Deer to Medicine Hat an endurance test.

The man might feel the necessity to talk, but Sasha felt absolutely no obligation to listen to him. She looked out the window and let her mind wander, consoling herself with the knowledge that this flight was definitely the quickest and therefore the best way to get home. Hearing the pilot's patter in the background was apparently the price she'd have to pay for that reward.

Today, being home sooner rather than later was important to Sasha. She wanted to tell her husband the exciting news— she had just found out she was pregnant! He'd always wanted to be a father and now, in a matter of months, he would be.

Just as she thought the word "father," she heard it, too, and the coincidence yanked her awareness back into the small plane and the pilot's nonstop conversation.

"Yeah, a lot of people don't believe me when I tell them that, but honestly, I did start flying as a kid. My father was a pilot. He owned a small plane, and for my tenth birthday, he took me flying. He flew out of an old airstrip just south of here. It's been abandoned for years, but back in the day we did a few 'touch and goes,' and then he let me have the controls. I'll never forget that. You know, I guess my father was my best friend. He died years ago, but I still miss him. He's the reason I became a pilot."

Sasha turned to look toward the man and nodded tentatively. Despite her best efforts, he was getting on her nerves.

"It's a bit weird that my father is on my mind so much this afternoon. It's probably just because I associate my dad with this area."

The man shifted in his seat and rubbed his eyes. Sasha noticed that his face was covered with a film of sweat. He couldn't be nervous, could he? He must have flown this route dozens if not hundreds of times.

"Say, Sasha—you don't mind if I call you by your first name, do you?" he asked, but didn't pause to give her a chance to reply. "You wouldn't happen to have any antacid tablets with you? I could sure use one. Got terrible heartburn for some reason."

Sasha fished in her briefcase until she came to the roll of Tums she kept there for emergencies. "One or two?" she asked.

"It's getting bad. Two for sure. No, wait, can you spare more, please? I'll replace them for you as soon as we're on the ground."

His voice had developed a shakiness that concerned Sasha. She held the unopened package toward him. He shook his head and mumbled something about not being able to open it himself. She ran her thumbnail across the folded foil, loosening the wrap. The pilot nodded slowly but didn't make a move to take any of the tablets. His head was turned away from her. He seemed to be looking out the window to his left.

"Dad, what are you doing here?" he said, slurring his words.

This dude's beginning to worry me, Sasha thought. "Hey!" she yelled. "Focus, would you please?"

"It's getting worse," he said, still slurring his words. "You gotta take over. Land this thing, will you?"

Sasha grabbed his shoulder and shook him. "Are you crazy? I can't fly a plane! What's wrong? Are you hallucinating? You're supposed to be flying this plane, remember? You can have your daydreams on someone else's dime!"

But the pilot didn't hear her. His lifeless body had slumped forward in his safety harness.

Sasha swore. She was terrified. The plane tilted to the right as it lost altitude faster than she would have believed possible.

"I'm gonna die. In seconds. Pregnant. In a plane crash. Seconds from now," she whimpered. Somehow not screaming felt important, and she pulled herself together. She might be about to die, but she'd do it with dignity.

Suddenly, a feeling of serenity infused the cockpit. Resigned, Sasha watched helplessly as the ground rushed up to meet her. Bile rising in her throat, she braced for the inevitable end, but at the last second, she felt the nose of the small plane tilt up. As it flew across the field, she could hear the top of the corn stalks brushing against the undercarriage, and then the sound stopped and she saw a clearing in front of her. The plane touched down and rolled almost to the end of the clearing before stopping, the engine coming to an idle.

Sasha jumped from the plane. As she stood looking around and trying to get her bearings, she realized that she was standing on a cracked and broken runway—the mere ghost of a long-abandoned airstrip.

THE SPORTS JACKET

Keith pressed down on the accelerator as he cleared the last bend in the S-curve. It was well after midnight, and there were no streetlights, but it was a warm summer's night and the sky was clear. Besides, if anyone knew the back roads of northern Manitoba, Keith did. In a minute, he'd be passing the old burial ground off to the left. That had always been a landmark for him—it meant that he was more than halfway home.

A movement in the bush at the side of the road caught his eye, and Keith slowed the car. He didn't need an animal jumping into the path of his car. He stared at the bush. Something was definitely making its way toward the road—a deer, perhaps?

No! That wasn't a deer. Whatever it was it stood upright. Keith's car fishtailed as he slammed on his brakes, but it was too late. A gut-wrenching thud shook the car, and he knew he'd hit something—a girl. He'd seen her clearly in the seconds before the impact. Throwing the shift into park, he jumped from the car and stood beside it, staring in disbelief.

He'd hit a girl—a girl or a young woman—either way, there was no question: he'd hit her and she was dead.

He bent down over the lifeless body, wailing in horror and disbelief at what he had done.

"I've gotta do something," he sobbed. "What, though? What? What? I can't just leave her here, lying dead in the middle of the road."

But nor could he bring himself to lift her into his car. "I've gotta go get help," he told himself, taking off his sports jacket and placing it carefully over the corpse.

As he drove to the nearest town, he tried to compose himself and think of the best way to explain what had happened. It sounded insane, but it was true—he'd been driving along a clear patch of roadway when a person had jumped out in front of his car and he'd hit her. That was exactly what had happened, so that was what he would say.

It wasn't hard to spot the police station: it was the only building in town with lights glowing in the windows. There was only one officer on duty, and he took the time to listen carefully to Keith's story.

"You'll be wanting a cup of tea to calm your nerves right about now, I'd imagine," the officer said kindly.

"Tea! We don't have time for tea." Keith's voice was strident. "We can't leave that poor girl's body lying on the road like that!"

"Have it your way, then," the officer said as he stood up and reached for his car keys. "But I think you'll be sorry that you didn't take me up on the offer of a warm drink. Never mind. We'll have it once we're back."

Keith shook with rage. He couldn't believe the disrespect this man was showing, not only to the poor, dead, young woman, but also indirectly to every other officer who had ever donned a uniform. This was just no way for a person in authority to behave.

The policeman drove slowly. In the passenger's seat, Keith leaned toward the windshield, his palms on the car's dashboard as if trying to push the cruiser to go faster.

"Stop the car!" Keith cried as they rounded the curve. "Right here. She jumped out in front of the car right here."

The first rays of what would soon become a glorious sunrise shone into the cruiser. The officer turned to Keith. "Before you get out of this car, there's something you need to know. You're not going to find a body out there in the middle of the road. You're not going to find anything at all. You're also probably never going to see your sports jacket again."

"You're crazy!" Keith shouted, throwing open the cruiser door and running to the spot where he had left the girl's body.

There was no body there.

"See? I was right," the policeman said with pride.

"She was here! I covered her with my jacket and left her here!"

"Son," the policeman said quietly, "what happened to you tonight has been happening on this stretch of road for more than fifty years that I know of—maybe for fifty more before that. Usually, the driver who hits her puts her in the back of his car and rushes to the local hospital, but when he arrives, the back seat is empty. She's vanished."

"Huh?"

"She's a ghost. You hit a ghost. People know about her; she's a spirit from the old cemetery, that's all. No one talks about it, and I'm sure that you won't either, but lots of people have hit her—or they thought they hit her. The question this time is what happened to your jacket."

Keith slouched against the hood of the cruiser. "The sun's coming up already. I need to walk this off—starting in that old burial ground."

"Have it your way, son. I'll put the kettle on when I get back to the station. You'll be needing a cup of tea by the time you get there."

Keith waited until the cruiser's taillights disappeared from view before stepping across the culvert and over the dilapidated fence that once neatly surrounded the graveyard. It was a sad sight. Most of the headstones were old and neglected. Some of them had even fallen over. Didn't anyone care about any of the people who were buried here?

Badly shaken, Keith wandered among the markers until he became overwhelmed. He stood still, closed his eyes, and wished blessings to all the departed souls buried there. When he opened his eyes, he felt better, strong enough to begin the long walk back to the police station to pick up his car. As he turned to leave the cemetery, he glanced down. There, folded neatly beside his feet, was his sports jacket. He picked it up. Underneath was a small, flat gravestone: "Sacred to the memory of Sarah Jean, 1832–1855."

"Rest in peace," Keith said, staring at the stone. Then he put on his jacket and made his way to the road. It was a long walk, but that was all right. He had a lot to think about. The one thing he knew for certain was that he would take that officer up on his offer of a cup of tea.

GHOSTS OF OAK ISLAND

If you've watched the television series *The Curse of Oak Island* about the current-day search for buried treasure on Oak Island, then you'll be up-to-date on how the treasure hunt is going, but the first ghost stories surrounding that island date back to well before anyone started to dig for any cache of valuables. And the ghost stories are even more interesting.

Oak Island is a small, peanut-shaped piece of land in Mahone Bay, Nova Scotia. European settlers first arrived in the area during the 1600s, but interestingly, of all the islands that dot the bay, the newcomers made a point of avoiding nearby Oak Island. As its name suggests, back in those days, the island was thick with a forest of oak trees, whereas all the other islands in the bay were covered in coniferous trees. Perhaps that difference made people wary.

But that oddity was only the beginning. Although there were no people living on Oak Island, lights danced at night through the oak trees and long shafts of light illuminated strange, shadowy shapes moving among the trees. Occasionally the settlers even heard disembodied voices echoing eerily through the trees. The settlers began to fear for their lives.

Two local men decided they would investigate this mystery that was frightening their neighbours. As the townsfolk watched nervously from shore, the two set out in a small rowboat. When the men steered the boat around the island and out of sight, their friends and family tried not to be concerned. After all, they knew that the island was small, so they were sure that the men in the rowboat would reappear from the other side in no time. Except they didn't. As a matter of fact, no trace of those brave men or as much as a splinter of their boat was ever seen again.

After that, Oak Island took on a deeply sinister reputation. It was an unnatural place, people said.

Then, in 1795, eighteen-year-old Daniel McGinnis decided to explore the dreaded island. He had heard that pirates sometimes buried their treasure on the many islands scattered around the bay, and McGinnis wanted to see if he could find some of those riches. He didn't, but what he did find changed the course of Oak Island's history, as well as the lives of generations of treasure hunters to come.

You see, in a small clearing on the island, McGinnis saw an odd depression in the land—a slumping, if you will. Then he noticed a scarred oak tree at the edge of that clearing. He took a second look. The marks on that tree had certainly not occurred naturally. It appeared that a branch of the tree had been used as a fulcrum for a pulley. Curious, he began to dig away at the earth.

To this day, the digging on Oak Island has not stopped. Today, the most sophisticated technology and the biggest machines available continue the treasure hunt that McGinnis started well more than a century and a quarter ago. In the intervening years, dozens of search companies have been formed. Families have moved to the island to live while they hunt for the rumoured treasure and, more often than not, those lives have been ruined. When or how the search will end is anyone's guess.

Some believe that the island is cursed and say that the elusive treasure will not be found until the oak trees that once covered the island are gone and until seven men have died trying to solve the mystery. Tragically, all of those requirements have been met. The oak trees have fallen victim to the relentless searching, and six treasure hunters have died under bizarre circumstances trying to get to the elusive cache of riches. The memory of those six men is honoured with a cairn, but there is no memorial to the two men who, in the 1600s, bravely rowed out to investigate the strange lights that were frightening their families. Their deaths bring the total number of lives lost in an effort to solve the Oak Island mystery to eight. The number of ghosts is much higher.

In the mid-1800s, a group of treasure hunters looked up from their shovels to see a strange cloud of vapour hovering just above the water near the island. Stranger still, the mist was moving toward them at a slow, steady pace. As the cloud came closer, the air around the searchers became colder and colder. Then a large rowboat that seemed to be making its way to the island appeared. The cloud evaporated, and the vision became clear. There were eight men in the boat, four on each side and each with an oar in his hand. The scene was so lifelike that the men on the island put down their tools and waved greetings.

One man even called out, inviting the boaters to come ashore. But as his words echoed across the bay, the eight men, and the boat they were rowing, vanished from sight.

Ironically, that apparition might have been the ghosts of the men who had buried the cache those searchers were after. For the rest of their lives, those searchers must have wondered whether, had they been silent, the phantoms might have come ashore and led them straight to the treasure.

Another ghostly encounter on the island indicates that might in fact have been so, because there are at least two tales from searchers who tell of a ghost appearing to them and informing the treasure hunters that they were not digging in the right place. There has been no word on whether or not the apparition redirected the men's efforts.

One winter, a little girl whose family was living on the island watched in awe as two men wearing red coats walked toward her. The child ran to tell her father about the visitors, but he could find no trace of the men—not even any tracks in the snow. Another time, a young boy out rowing in the bay was terrified when he, too, saw the ghosts dressed in red coats. From the children's descriptions and the era in which the sightings occurred, many people think that those were the ghosts of soldiers in the British army, who would have been on the island to defend the land against capture by the French.

At this writing, the mysteries of Nova Scotia's Oak Island remain, perhaps guarded by its many ghosts.

THE PAINTING

Diane had loved her time in the north, and she didn't want to leave without a souvenir of her stay in Iqaluit. The afternoon before she was scheduled to fly home to Flin Flon, Manitoba, she set out to find herself a keepsake to remind her of the visit. When she happened upon a small oil painting in a gift shop, she knew she'd found exactly what she wanted. Even so, she hesitated a moment before buying it because she and her husband, Paul, had completely different tastes in art. She didn't think that he would like her choice.

And she was right.

"That's the ugliest painting I've ever seen in my life," he told her when she showed him the painting. "You aren't hoping to hang that thing anywhere in our house, are you?"

"It's not ugly," Diane had retorted. "It's sophisticated, and yes, I most certainly am going to hang it in the house. There's a perfect spot for it in the dining room."

"The dining room? Well, make sure it's not on a wall that I can see from where I sit at the table. I'll choke if I have to look at that while I'm eating. That's not art—it's appalling. I mean, look at it. What is it? It's a solid black background with a big black silhouette of a house. There's nothing even interesting about that. Who wants an all-black painting?"

Diane sighed. "I do, obviously, and anyway, it's not all black. It's a nighttime scene, and you're right, the house is a silhouette, but see up there in the corner? There's a tiny light shining through the attic window. That's the part of the picture I like the best."

Several months later, Paul still occasionally grumbled about Diane's taste in artwork, but for the most part, the issue had been dropped and they had gone on with their lives.

One day, they were planning a dinner party.

"We'll keep it small so that it's intimate," Diane suggested.

Paul rolled his eyes, but Diane continued to explain her plans. "If we just invite two other couples, we can serve the meal formally, in the dining room."

"Yeah, okay, but don't change my place at the table. If you do, you'd better take the painting down. Where I sit now is the only chair in the room where you can't see that black beast."

Diane nodded. She had no intention of taking down the painting or changing Paul's seat at the dining room table, but she had every intention of hosting a nice get-together.

Predictably, the dinner guests all commented on the painting. It was eye-catching, which was one of the reasons Diane had been attracted to it in the first place. When her friend's husband commented that the picture was all black, she jumped to the artist's defence.

"But it isn't! If you look carefully at the dark house, you'll see that there's a light shining through the attic window,"

Diane said as she walked toward the painting with her arm extended, ready to point out her favourite feature of the piece.

But the light wasn't shining. There was no light anywhere in the painting. It was, indeed, all black.

Diane's temper did a slow burn all through dinner. Paul must have painted over the yellowy glow in the window of the house. He'd occasionally played practical jokes on her, but this wasn't even a little bit funny. This was vandalism, and when their company left that evening, she told him so in no uncertain terms. Of course, he pleaded complete innocence, but how else could it have happened?

They stared at one another as the atmosphere between them chilled to frosty. It was clear that they were giving one another the silent treatment. Neither one was about to give an inch, to the point that when the phone rang later that evening they both ignored it. It wasn't until seven thirty the following morning, when Diane was clearing the voicemail, that they learned one of their dinner guests of the previous night had suffered a fatal heart attack while driving home.

It took fully a month for Paul and Diane's life to return to normal. During the mental and emotional turmoil of coming to grips with their friend's death, they each promised to themselves to treat the other with more respect and kindness—which is why when Diane noticed that the light in the painting was once again shining through the attic window like a beacon of hope, she was touched by Paul's thoughtful gesture of repair. Oddly, when she tried to thank him for touching up the tiny spot on the painting, he denied doing it as vehemently as he had when she had accused him of painting over it. After that, neither one of them ever mentioned the painting again.

By the end of summer, they were both feeling that the pain of their friend's death had healed a bit and that it would be good to invite some people over for a meal.

"Let's make this a family occasion," Diane suggested. "How about just your parents and mine?"

"We're not serving any booze, then—not even wine," Paul said firmly. "You know my father. Once he gets started, he just doesn't stop and he gets totally obnoxious."

Diane agreed immediately. Paul's mother was a fine woman, but his father, well, he was fine too, unless he was drinking. Alcohol would get the best of that man eventually, she was sure.

The night of the family dinner, Diane set the table carefully. She put out her good wineglasses in anticipation of serving a sweet sparkling cider that she'd bought. This is going to be a good evening, she thought as she stood back and glanced over the room.

And then she saw it: the painting! The painting was all black again! There was no light shining through the attic window. How could Paul do something like that? He must have known it would upset her. Honestly, his sense of humour could be so tasteless.

Diane stormed into the kitchen, ready to lace into her husband, but he was talking on the telephone and clearly the conversation was not going well. He hung up, turned to her, and said, "That was my mom. It's about Dad. He went to the liquor store to buy some wine to bring to the party tonight. Someone ran a red light. Dad's dead."

INVISIBLE PRESENCE

It was January when Eric finally found himself a job in a small town in northern British Columbia. He'd been unemployed for so long that he'd have gone almost anywhere to find work. For the first week he was there, he took a room at the local hotel, but the room rates were draining what little savings he had. He needed to find a much cheaper place to live, but accommodations nearby were scarce. Fortunately, a workmate told him about a small house for rent just at the edge of town. Eric gave the landlord a deposit and moved in that evening.

The house consisted of one large room on the main floor with a rickety old ladder leading to a low attic, where there was an uncomfortable-looking cot. *It's cheap, so this will have to be home for a while,* Eric told himself as he unpacked his few belongings and got ready to bunk down for the night. He had to be at work by six in the morning.

He slept fitfully and woke up feeling more tired than when he'd gone to bed. He had no choice but to get up, though, because he'd been warned that if he clocked in even one minute later than six, his pay would be docked. At least he knew he'd be heading back to his new home in the early afternoon; a very appealing thought on a number of fronts, partly because it would be the first time he'd see his new home in daylight.

At the end of his shift, Eric was so tired on his way home that even the creaky metal cot crammed into the tiny attic with its low ceilings held some appeal.

As he rounded the corner and the house came into sight, his heart sank. The place looked like a dump. The last time that building had been painted, Trudeau must've been prime minister—Pierre Trudeau, that is, not Justin. Worse, there was only one tiny round window in the front of the house, a porthole in the attic. *Please don't let this be my sinking ship,* Eric thought.

His shoulders slumping, the dejected, dog-tired man unlocked the front door and stepped inside—and stopped dead in his tracks. There was someone in the house. He could feel their presence. He called out "Hello!" but no one answered. He drew in as deep a breath as he could and moved one foot in front of the other before calling out again, more loudly this time. Still no one answered.

It's just my nerves from lack of sleep, Eric told himself as he walked quickly to the kitchen area at the back of the room. *I'll make myself a cup of tea and a sandwich. That'll settle my nerves,* he thought.

As he poured water into a battered old kettle, he stared out the grimy kitchen window. *What?* The man could hardly believe his eyes. There was an even smaller house not ten metres behind his! He rubbed his sleeve against the window to get a better view. Yes, there it was: not much more than a shack, really, but it was there, a house with a door and a window facing Eric's window and back door. *No wonder the rent for this place is so low,* he thought. *The landlord has two houses on one small yard.*

At least that annoyance took his mind off the sensation of not being alone in the house—until he heard footsteps walking across the floor upstairs. Gathering his courage, Eric climbed a few steps up on the ladder to investigate. As soon as his head was through the opening on the attic floor, he looked around. There was nothing there except the small bed he'd tried to sleep on the night before.

Besides, how could anyone have been walking across this floor? You can't even stand up straight up here, except in the middle, he thought, trying to convince himself that his imagination was playing tricks on him. He looked around more carefully to reassure himself that all was well.

And that was when he heard the footsteps again, this time coming from downstairs. He squeezed his eyes closed and clamped his hands on the ladder's rungs. *What's going on?*

All Eric knew for certain was that he had to get out of that house, even if that meant facing whoever or whatever was in there with him. Step by step, as quietly as he could, the terrified man backed his way down the few rungs to the floor downstairs.

In the few moments he'd been on the ladder, the temperature in the downstairs room had become icy cold. *It feels colder inside than it is outside,* Eric thought as he watched his breath form clouds of mist in the empty room.

Calm down, fella, he told himself. *You don't need to go running out. Nothing's really happened. It's all just your imagination.* Even so, he put his jacket and boots back on to fight off the cold before starting to make himself something to eat and drink. As he did, Eric glanced out the window again and, much to his surprise, saw a man standing in the doorway of the house behind him.

The man was wearing pajamas with a housecoat hanging loose around his shoulders. Relieved to have some human contact, Eric opened the back door and waved to the man, who immediately did up the belt on his housecoat. *I've gotta go over there and talk to the guy. Maybe he knows something about this house.*

Eric walked the few steps between the two houses and introduced himself to his neighbour.

"Matthew," the man replied.

"We really are next-door neighbours, aren't we?" Eric said, indicating how close the houses were to one another.

The two men stood chatting for a few moments. Just as Eric was getting up his nerve to ask if Matthew had any information about his new digs, the man asked him a question. "Don't you have to be getting back to your company?"

"Company?

"Your guest. I saw someone standing behind you when you waved to me. I didn't have my glasses on, so I couldn't make out whether it was a man or a woman, but there was definitely someone there."

Eric tried to explain what had been happening in the house, but all that came out of his mouth was a jumble of words that really made no sense. Finally he managed to ask Matthew to stay at his doorway and watch while Eric went back into the larger of the two houses. "When I get back inside, I'll wave to you. Wave back if you see anything unusual."

And so Matthew did. In the few seconds it took for Eric to get inside to the window, his new neighbour was waving both arms frantically over his head. "Someone went into the house right after you!" he yelled.

Eric fled back to the hotel, where he stayed until the next day, when he could get a bus back to his hometown. He hated the thought of being unemployed again, but he hated the thought of living in a haunted house even more.

MIDWIFE OR SOOTHSAYER?

It was a dreadful night in Montreal on February 20, 1896.

If you've ever been to that fine city during February, you'll know exactly how nasty those winter nights can be, with wind howling around the corners outside and blowing snow crystals as sharp as daggers that cut into your exposed flesh.

Inside Antoinette and Carl Hartley's humble home, a single lantern burned; its flame had flickered, it seemed, with each one of Antoinette's screams of pain. The midwife, Madame Madelaine Donat, now stood at the woman's bedside while Carl tenderly held his strong and healthy newborn son, but the new mother was still in great distress.

"What's wrong?" Carl asked Madame Donat. "The baby is born! Please, do something to help my wife."

The midwife probed the woman's abdomen and smiled. "Antoinette, you are doubly blessed. Mother Nature is giving you a nice surprise."

With that, the Hartleys' daughter was born, as strong and healthy as her twin brother. The new parents sat in stunned silence, each cradling a tiny baby. At first, so taken by the beauty of their son and daughter, neither of them noticed that

Madame Donat had walked across the room and was sitting at the table, making notes, presumably a record of the births.

Once the infants were both fast asleep, the Hartleys looked over at the midwife, who was still scribbling furiously at the table.

"Perhaps she's leaving us a list of instructions about how to care for the babies," Carl suggested.

"She must have a great deal to tell us," Antoinette replied. "Thank goodness she was able to make it here on time through that dreadful storm."

Carl wiped his wife's brow with a damp cloth and then took a hesitant step across the room toward Madame Donat. The woman's breathing was heavy, and she was muttering to herself as she wrote. When she sensed the new father standing beside her, she gave an exaggerated sigh, threw down the pen, and stood up.

"You'll be needing to take good care of your wife, Mr. Hartley. And those babies need regular feedings around the clock," the woman said. "I'll be back to check on all of you sometime tomorrow. All will be well, God willing."

The Hartleys thanked the woman profusely and sincerely. They truly didn't know what they would've done without the midwife's help. But now they were anxious to have her leave so that they could see what it was she'd been writing all that time.

Carl went to the table and picked up the only book that the couple had ever had in their house—the family Bible. He opened the cover, but at first couldn't see any handwritten words. He flipped to the inside of the back cover, and that's when he saw the midwife's notation:

I attest and bear my sign and seal herewith and duly record that on the 20th day in February, in the year of our Lord, 1896, I have delivered of Mrs. Antoinette Hartley and her husband, Mr. Carl Hartley, one fine baby boy and one fine baby girl. The son and the daughter are healthy and sound and do not bear any marks or deformity. The son is to be called Carl Gerald. The daughter is to be called Edith Anne. I predict that they shall live extraordinary lives for three score and eight years and that they shall be blessed with the higher powers of God until the hour of five upon the fifth day of the fifth month, at which time one will call upon the other to withdraw from this Earth. So be it that this birth record and document shall forever attest to what I, the undersigned hath writ here:

*Her Hand and Seal at Montreal, Quebec
Madelaine Donat, Midwife.*

Antoinette recoiled in horror. "The woman who delivered our babies is a soothsayer. She is evil."

"Eccentric, she's eccentric. I'll give you that, my dear wife and mother of my beautiful children."

"She defaced our Bible. I will not have her in our home ever again," Antoinette cried.

The parents' heated conversation disturbed their newborn daughter. Antoinette rocked the infant and whispered, "Edith Anne, be at peace." Then she looked up at Carl. "Did you tell

Madame Donat what names we'd chosen in case the baby was a daughter?"

"No, I'm sure we didn't," he replied.

"Then how could she have known that we would call her Edith Anne?"

The colour drained from Carl's face. He knew for a fact that neither of them had mentioned names for the babies. Guessing that a son might be named after him wasn't too much of a stretch, but Edith Anne was a name they had chosen simply because they liked the sound of the two words together. How could Madame Donat have known? Suddenly he realized that the midwife who had attended to his wife and infants was one who was gifted with second sight. He took the Bible and hid it in the bottom of a drawer that was seldom used.

Carl Gerald and Edith Anne grew up with love and were always so close to one another that it was almost as if they shared a mind—or perhaps were "blessed with the higher powers of God," as Madame Donat had predicted at their birth.

As an adult, Edith Anne married a wealthy coal baron and moved to Pennsylvania. Carl Gerald soon took a job in his brother-in-law's mine. One afternoon, a vicious fire broke out in the coal pit. Carl Gerald and his co-workers were trapped.

At home, Edith Anne suddenly jumped to her feet. "There's a fire," she declared urgently. "Carl Gerald and the others need help."

Edith Anne's husband gathered as many helpers as he could find and hurried to the mine. They arrived just in time and managed to save all the miners. If it hadn't been for Edith

Anne's sudden vision, the fire would most certainly have been fatal.

Some years later, Carl Gerald travelled back to Montreal to visit their mother. The moment he walked in the door, he knew she was critically ill—and so did his twin sister, even though she was at her home in Pennsylvania, hundreds of miles away. Edith Anne had packed a suitcase and was about to board a train for Canada. Sadly, the twins' mother died shortly after her daughter's arrival.

While Edith Anne was happily married, her twin brother remained a bachelor until the year he decided to do some travelling around his adopted home country of the United States of America. While he was in California, he met a woman and fell in love with her. Although Carl Gerald intended to keep the news as a surprise for his sister, Edith Anne, who was at home in Pennsylvania, knew about the wedding as it was happening.

Some years later, in June 1963, Edith Anne was suffering with a restless mood. She had paced back and forth the entire morning, and nothing seemed able to calm her. Then, as she stood at her bedroom window, a vision came to her, like a movie being played in slow motion. She watched in horror as her mind's eye showed her a car crash on a California highway. Once again, she knew her brother's life was in jeopardy. She drove to the airport and boarded a plane to California, where she found both her brother and his wife in the hospital with severe injuries after a car accident. Edith Anne stayed with them and helped nurse them both until they were finally able to look after themselves again.

So it would seem that the twins did indeed have "the higher powers of God," just as Madelaine Donat, the midwife, had prophesied. The next year, on May 5, 1964, at 5:00 AM Eastern Daylight Time, the final episode in her prophecy played out.

Edith Anne was awakened at home with pains in her chest. She tried to waken her husband, but he slept deeply and she couldn't rouse him. She struggled to her feet and managed to take two steps before falling hard against the night table beside the bed, knocking down the lamp and a full glass of water.

Her husband called out groggily to her, but she didn't answer him. Instead she cried out, "Oh dear Lord, Carl Gerald is dead!"

Her husband got up and rushed to his wife's side to see what had happened, but the room was dark. He fumbled for the lamp and cursed when the switch wouldn't work.

"Here," Edith Anne uttered weakly. The lamp cord had wrapped itself around her arm as she'd fallen. The glass of water had spilled, but fortunately, the glass had not broken or she might have been seriously cut. She managed to unwind the cord from her arm and plug the lamp into the wall socket. Less than a second later, a flash of blue illuminated the room. Dainty puffs of smoke rose from the metal rollers she had used to set her hair the night before. Her fingers, wet from the spilled water, had touched the plug, and she lay dead on her bedroom floor—electrocuted.

Moments later and thousands of kilometres away in California, Carl Gerald's wife knelt beside his limp body. He had died of a heart attack.

And so it was that one twin had indeed called the other to "withdraw from this Earth," on the fifth hour of the fifth day of the fifth month, just as the midwife had predicted three score and eight years earlier.

WAIFS

Ah, the Internet—how it's changed the lives of humankind! Perhaps the old saying is true, though: The more things change, the more they stay the same. For instance, bizarre stories about creatures who never die but walk the earth forever in search of their sustenance—human blood. Their disguises have changed over the years from beautiful women with long, pointed incisor teeth to Hollywood's Bella Lugosi sort, with a red-lined black cape wrapped around him like a bat's wings. These days, characters like this and their exploits are all over the Internet.

Some think that today's incarnations of these unnatural beasts are posing as children: skinny little waifs nearly as thin as toothpicks, with dirty faces and rags for clothes. They keep their faces downcast so no one will see their blank expressions or vacant eyes. Like all creatures with ill intent, it's said that they prey on those who are most vulnerable. Someone like eight-year-old Joey, who happened to be alone in his house in Winnipeg for the first time ever one morning when he heard something pounding on the front door. The noise startled him, especially as no one ever came to the front door—not unless there was some sort of trouble, that is.

Hesitantly, the child opened the inside door and peered through the screen door, noticing with relief that it was tightly latched.

Two dirty, skinny lads stood on the small porch. The taller of the two, who was about Joey's height, gave a half-wave and said something that sounded like "Hey, kid."

"What do you want?" Joey asked.

"Well, we think it'd be right neighbourly of you if you invited us both in for a cold drink. It's mighty hot out here in the sun," the same boy said.

For a moment, Joey felt sympathetic. It *was* hot out there. The heat wave that had started last week still hadn't broken. But sympathy aside, he didn't even feel safe with these kids at the door, and he sure didn't want to let them inside. He shook his head and started to close the door.

"Wait!" It was the tall skinny kid again. The smaller one was even skinnier. He hadn't spoken at all. "Okay then, just open the door. We want to show you something."

"What do you want to show me?" Joey asked.

"It'll be a surprise. You'll like it," the taller kid said. The smaller one kept his head down but nodded in agreement with his companion.

These kids are freaky, Joey thought. *The taller one's so skinny he must be light as a feather, but his voice sounds like an adult's.*

"I can see whatever it is through the screen," Joey said.

"You're nothing but a baby," the tall kid taunted. "A scaredy cat."

Joey stepped back, ready to close the door.

"Wait a minute!" the tall kid yelled, his voice sounding like Joey's father's when he lost his temper.

Joey peered out through the screen door once again. Both kids were staring at him with their blank faces and dull eyes. Suddenly a wave of loneliness swept over Joey, and he thought maybe it would be nice to have some company, even if these boys were kind of weird. He could invite them in and show them his new Hot Wheels. He reached out to lift the latch on the screen door just as he heard the back door swing open and his mother call his name. Then she added, "Joey, come help me bring in the groceries."

"Let us in!" the taller kid snarled. The shorter kid's fingernails dug into the screen door, leaving ten uneven rips in the webbing.

Joey slammed the front door and locked it. He'd never been so glad to carry groceries from his mother's car. If he told his mother that he'd opened the door to strangers, he'd be in big trouble, so he didn't say a word about the scrawny, bossy kids.

After all the bags full of groceries were on the kitchen counter, Joey's mother thanked him for his help and asked if he'd like to go with her to Grandma's house in Brandon this afternoon.

"Yes," he said before she barely had the words out of her mouth.

His mom affectionately mussed Joey's hair. "It makes me happy that you're so fond of your grandma."

Joey did love his grandmother, but today her house was extra appealing just because it was somewhere else to be—that is, out of Winnipeg and away from those menacing-looking kids who were lurking around.

Grandma had baked his favourite gingerbread cookies. While his mother and grandmother chatted and Joey enjoyed an entire plateful of cookies, he couldn't help thinking about those skinny kids who'd been at the door that morning. They didn't look as though they'd ever had a grandmother—or anyone else for that matter—bake cookies for them.

As the afternoon at Grandma's went along, the peculiar little strangers who'd been at the door that morning began to fade from his mind, and when his grandmother asked Joey if he'd like to stay overnight at her house, the boy jumped at the chance. His mother smiled and nodded, once again thoroughly enjoying the obvious fondness between her son and her mother.

That night, Joey had trouble falling asleep. He kept thinking he heard fingernails ripping against the screen on the bedroom window. When he finally did doze off, he was tormented by nightmares of skinny kids ordering him around with angry, adult voices.

The next morning he felt terrible; his eyes were hot and scratchy, and the sides of his neck were red and itchy. *Grandma's pancakes and her soft voice will fix everything,* he told himself.

But Joey was wrong.

There were no pancakes, and Grandma's voice was not soft.

"It's about time you finally woke up, you lazy bag of bones," Grandma screamed at him. "Those two skinny friends of yours were here to call on you hours ago."

Joey's pulse pounded in his ears. "Did you let them in?" he asked, his voice shaking.

"Let them in? Of course I let them in! They looked like they hadn't had a decent meal in months. Pathetic little waifs, so they were. Mighty grateful to get your stack of pancakes, I'll tell you."

"Oh." Joey's voice was barely audible.

"They were so polite and nice, it made my head swoon. Have yourself a bowl of cereal if you want to. I need to go lie down on the couch. I'm feeling a little dizzy."

As Joey watched his grandmother make her way the few short steps from the kitchen into the living room, he noticed she had two streaks of blood running down each side of her neck.

Perhaps the ancient villainous creatures of folklore are still with us, and only their disguises have changed. At least, that's what some forums on the Internet would have us believe.

MOST HAUNTED HOUSE IN CANADA?

Our homes are where we go to feel safe and protected from the world—but what if you share that space with a presence you don't understand?

When Monica and Philippe bought their first house in a lovely little town in southern Ontario, they were as happy as a young couple could be. The house was a real bargain, and they felt very fortunate to be able to afford to buy the place, especially as Monica was pregnant with their first child and they wanted to be settled in time for the birth. The person who sold it to them hadn't mentioned that there was a reason for the low price. He hadn't even told them that three other couples had tried to live there in the space of only a couple of years—or that the house had stood vacant for a number of months.

"The house was on a pretty street," Philippe remembered. "The boulevards were lined with mature maple trees and the house itself was tall and stately."

That part wasn't a surprise, since a well known architect had built the house for his own family. The house had stayed in that family for three generations, only changing hands when the man's spinster granddaughter died and the place went up for sale for the first time.

The couple was so pleased to be in their first home that even unpacking boxes felt like a treat—until Philippe sensed someone standing so close beside him that he could feel the breath on his neck. He looked up, expecting to see Monica, but there was no one there—no one that he could see, that is. He shrugged his shoulders and went on with the job at hand. Little did he know that the feeling of someone being near him when he could plainly see that no one was there was a sensation he'd soon become accustomed to.

A few days later, Philippe bought himself a new lawn mower and, with great pride, began to cut the lawn around their new home. He was singing to himself when the lawn mower gave a sudden jolt that ran up his arms. The wheels had caught in a small depression in the ground. Curious, he turned off the mower and hauled a shovel out from the garden shed. He dug down nearly a metre but didn't find any reason for the hollow. Then, having dug the hole, he decided that he might as well start personalizing the landscaping by planting a tree.

One of their favourite rooms in the house was the living room. It could be closed off from the rest of the house by French doors that opened with lovely old glass doorknobs. The centrepiece of the living room was a huge fieldstone fireplace. In the evenings, the couple would often light a fire and sit together to chat about the excitement of becoming parents for the first time. Most nights, Monica would go upstairs to bed earlier than Philippe, leaving him to put the fire out and close the chimney flue and the fire screen, leaving the hot ashes in the hearth until morning.

One morning, Philippe was awake and downstairs before his wife. As he walked past the fireplace, he was startled to see that although the flue and the screen were still closed, the ashes from the hearth had been swept into a neat pile in front of the fireplace. He turned around to make sure he was alone in the room, and as he did, he watched in awe as the French doors closed by themselves and the glass doorknobs turned.

Even though Monica was pregnant, Philippe knew he would have to tell her about this. Much to his surprise, his wife was relieved to have the discussion, because she, too, had felt as though there was something strange about the house. She added that she had even heard party sounds coming from everywhere and nowhere. Whenever it happened, she would go through the whole house to try and find where the sounds were coming from, but the source eluded her every time. She'd even heard the front door open and close, followed by the sounds of footsteps going up the staircase. Monica had been so sure of what she heard that she'd called out to her husband each time, but each time he hadn't been nearby.

And so it was that they both knew there was something very peculiar about this place where they had planned to raise their family. Although they didn't discuss them, the incidents were never far from their minds.

Once their daughter was born, they were too tired and preoccupied to notice most ordinary events, much less extraordinary ones.

When the little girl was a few months old, Monica and some friends went out for dinner, leaving Philippe to handle the bedtime routine. He fed the baby, changed her into her sleepers, and sat with the child in his arms as he rocked her to sleep. Just as he was about to set the baby down for the night, her crib lifted off the floor and slammed back down again. Then it happened again and again and again.

Holding the banister to help support his shaky legs, Philippe carried the sleeping infant downstairs, where the two of them fell asleep in front of the television. The next day, he moved the baby's crib into the spare room and the crib never moved again, although both new parents often felt that unseen presence when they were with the baby and even heard what they thought sounded like a woman sighing.

Fortunately, whatever spirit was haunting their house wasn't tormenting the baby. It did, however, break up a dinner party they were hosting once when one of their guests suddenly stood up from the table and ran outside, leaving the others to wonder what the problem could be. When Philippe talked to his friend later, the man told him that he'd suddenly felt extremely cold and that someone was breathing down his neck. Philippe and Monica felt they needed to explain to their guest that they suspected the house was haunted.

After they did, the frightened man's wife suggested that they get to the bottom of the supernatural mystery with automatic writing, adding that spirits would sometimes communicate with the living through that medium. Then the woman demonstrated the technique by sitting at the table with a pen poised over a piece of paper. After a few minutes, her hand started to move, but only to draw a few squiggly lines. Philippe and then Monique were the next to try the experiment. Philippe's hand eventually drew one straight line, and Monica's hand didn't move at all.

Feeling calmer, the man who had run from the house took the pen and a fresh sheet of paper. Seconds later, as clear as could be, was a single word: DEVIL.

Monica knew it was time to move away from their once-beloved home, but Philippe was still curious. He hired a psychic to come to the house. "I see an older woman sitting at an old-fashioned treadle sewing machine," the woman told him. At least that gave him some insight into who the ghost might be. The next day, they listed the house for sale.

The first prospective buyer to look at the house was a woman who had grown up just across the street from it. She told the couple that the spinster who'd lived alone in the house for decades had a series of cats that she loved dearly.

"I remember," she told Philippe and Monica, "that as each one died, she buried it on the property. The last one was buried just where you planted that tree."

The couple stared. They were speechless. The woman continued. "The old lady would warn us kids never to disturb the cats' resting places."

Philippe could hardly believe his ears. If only he hadn't dug that small hole in the lawn the first week they lived here, all of this might have been avoided.

Even so, the house was for sale, and they were ready to move on. The place sold quickly. They heard later that the new owners had brought in an exorcist before they moved in.

And they never planted any more trees on the property.

AFTERWORD

Hello to you, my extra-curious campers! I'm so glad you're here to find out which stories in this book are based on actual events. Eight of the stories in *Campfire Stories from Coast to Coast* are based on fact. Read on and find out which ones.

"CAPTURED"

Believe it or not, this story is purported to be true. The man I called "Bert" was Albert Ostman. In 1957, Mr. Ostman wrote a letter to a newspaper in Agassiz, BC, recounting an astonishing experience with a family of sasquatches that had taken place in 1924. He had never spoken of his ordeal before, but in the late 1950s, there had been a flurry of local interest in sasquatches, and Ostman felt he should reveal his encounter with the family of beasts. The story is well covered in a book called *Abominable Snowmen: Legend Come to Life*, written by Ivan T. Sanderson and published by Pyramid Books in 1968.

"THE *EMPRESS OF IRELAND*"

This story is based on a tragic historical event. According to *The Canadian Encyclopedia*, the *Empress of Ireland* was an "ocean-going passenger ship that sank in the St. Lawrence

River near Rimouski, Quebec [on] 29 May 1914. She was rammed in dense fog by the Norwegian collier [coal-carrying ship] *Storstad* and sank in fourteen minutes; 1014 passengers and crew died, while 465 managed to abandon ship. Bodies recovered from the *Empress* were gathered in the village of Ste-Luce and buried near Metis-sur-Mer, where a monument stands to their memory. Captain Anderson of the *Storstad* was later held responsible for the disaster." The *Storstad* was called into service during the First World War and sank during a battle in 1917.

Jerome Stout was indeed the postmaster on the remote Scottish island of Fair Isle. His terrifying awareness of the disaster when he was sitting quietly in church, thousands of kilometres away, was duly recorded that Sunday. There is no indication that Stout ever experienced clairvoyance again.

"GHOST HILL"

The various components that make up this story are always told as true, and even today, the haunting is often blamed for car accidents that occur on that winding, hilly section of road.

"AN UNSOLVED MYSTERY"

The story of the *Ellen Austin* is absolutely true—up to a point. Captain Baker and his crew did come across an abandoned schooner as they were approaching Newfoundland, and he did attempt to haul it to port in order to claim her for salvage. To that end, Baker ordered some of his men to board the mysterious, unidentified vessel and to sail her close behind the *Ellen Austin*, but then a storm blew up, making visibility so poor that the two ships lost sight of one another. When the weather cleared, the mysterious schooner could again be seen, but the men Baker had ordered on board had vanished. All of that information has been officially documented.

Let's hope that the "facts" of the story from that point on are fiction. The information comes from the writings of a retired British Royal Navy officer named Gould in 1944. Gould maintained that the *Ellen Austin*'s Captain Baker wanted the salvage profits so badly that he ordered a second group of sailors to board the abandoned ship. It's hard (and awful!) to imagine that this is true, considering the men Baker had already lost to the ill-fated vessel, and even more difficult to imagine those sailors obeying that order.

"THE LAST SEASON"

Readers with an interest in hockey history or a fondness for the Tragically Hip song "Fifty Mission Cap" may find this story familiar. On April 21, 1951, during the seventh game of the Stanley Cup finals against the Montreal Canadiens, Toronto Maple Leafs defenceman Bill Barilko scored an overtime goal to win the Cup for his team. Four months after the victory, Barilko and a friend celebrated with a fly-in fishing trip to an isolated lake in northern Ontario. The pair never returned. It was as if the Leafs hero and his friend had vanished. A search was launched, but to no avail. In the meantime, eleven hockey seasons came and went, but the Toronto Maple Leafs did not win the Stanley Cup again until 1962, when the wreckage of a small plane was found in a heavily forested area near Cochrane, Ontario. The remains of Bill Barilko and his friend were inside.

This story is an important part of Canadian historical lore and, sadly, all the deaths mentioned have occurred. As for the ghosts—how could a place with a past such as Oak Island has had not be haunted?

"EXTRATERRESTRIAL VISIT"

While this story is fictional, there was an encounter at Falcon Lake, Manitoba, on May 20, 1967, which remains controversial to this day. Stefan Michalak's experience with an unidentified flying object has been documented in the book *When They Appeared: Falcon Lake 1967: The inside story of a close encounter*, written by Stefan's son, Stan Michalak, and Chris Rutkowski, who is generally accepted as being the most knowledgeable UFO expert in Canada.

"MIDWIFE OR SOOTHSAYER?"

According to Robert Tralins's book *ESP Forewarnings*, the Hartleys' family Bible that contained the midwife's inscription was found among Carl Gerald Hartley's possessions following his death. Along with the Bible were several journals documenting the strange events of the twins' lives and a note that Edith Anne had never known about the midwife's prophecy.

In days gone by, midwives were often believed to be witches with special powers. In this case, it would seem that the midwife, Madelaine Donat, certainly did have abilities that went well beyond the realm of ordinary folk medicine and included the ability to accurately predict the future.

It would be interesting to know, of all the births she must have attended, how many people later discovered a strange, prophetic inscription in their family Bible.

"ROOM FOR ONE MORE"

According to sociologist Dr. Barrie W. Robinson (1944–2011), "This story is an excellent example of an urban legend, an oft-told tale that supposedly serves some kind of purpose. What would be the purpose of an urban legend? We can assume that legends are no more than the modern equivalent of old-time morality or cautionary tales. These tales seem to have been designed to enforce informal social control (as opposed to the formal systems of social control such as laws) and of reinforcing informal norms of conduct. Morality or cautionary tales recount what happens to people who violate informal norms (never anything good!) and, by negative example, extol the virtues of following the straight-and-narrow."

Variations of "Room for One More—A Cautionary Tale" have been around for more than a century. The oldest published version was way back in 1906, when the *Pall Mall Magazine* ran a short story by E.F. Benson called "The Bus Conductor." In most retellings, a central figure—usually a bus conductor or an elevator operator—indicates there is only room for one more person. Because of our hero's dreams or premonitions, they shy away from taking that last spot and thereby save their own life.

If this is a cautionary tale, it probably serves to direct us away from the evil creatures that might live in our minds. While such caution might postpone our demise, in reality we all know that although we might be able to postpone death, eventually the grim reaper—or bus conductor or elevator operator in this case—will surely get us all in the end.

"WAIFS" AND "VILLAGE VISITOR"

Now I know that you really, really want those vampire stories to be true, but you're in for a disappointment—I totally made them up. Sorry!

ACKNOWLEDGEMENTS

Thanks to everyone at Heritage House for sharing their talents with my projects, and special thanks to Rodger Touchie for embracing my suggestion for this volume. Thank you to Karla Decker for once again improving my work with her editing skills. You're such a pleasure to work with.

Jacqui Thomas did an extraordinary job on the book's layout and design. Thank you, Jacqui. And thank you to Nandini Thaker, whose prompt efficiency and friendly support were so helpful. Many thanks, also, to Lesley Cameron for her amazing proofreading skills.

Much love and appreciation to those closest to me, my friends and family, and especially Bob, my support in life and resident proofreader!

Thank you to booksellers for all the support you've given my work over the years. And thanks to you, too, my readers. Without you, there would be no point in any author writing any book.

BIBLIOGRAPHY

Bauchman, Rosemary. *Mysteries and Marvels: Incredible Happenings from Near and Far.* Hants Port, NS: Lancelot Press, 1991.

Christensen, Jo-Anne. *Ghosts, Werewolves, Witches and Vampires.* Edmonton, AB: Lone Pine Publishing, 2001.

Lanternhead, Kayak. *Cape Breton Island Campfire Stories: Horrifying Fables for Your Next Camping Trip.* Scotts Valley, CA: CreateSpace Publishing (amazon.com), 2016.

Michalak, Stan, and Chris Rutkowski. *When They Appeared: Falcon Lake 1967: The inside story of a close encounter.* Winnipeg, MB: McNally Robinson, 2017.

Myers, Arthur, Margaret Rau, and John Macklin. *The Little Giant Book of "True" Ghost Stories.* New York, NY: Sterling Publishing Co., 1998.

Sanderson, Ivan T. *Abominable Snowmen: Legend Come to Life.* Publishing location unknown: Pyramid Books, 1968.

S.E. Schlosser, *Spooky Canada, Tales of Hauntings, Strange Happenings and Other Local Lore.* Guilford, CT: Insiders' Guide, 2007.

The Canadian Encyclopedia. Edmonton, AB: Hurtig Publishers Ltd., 1988.

Tralins, Robert, *ESP Forewarnings.* New York, NY: Popular Library, 1969.

ABOUT THE AUTHOR

Barbara Smith was born and raised in Toronto and lived most of her life in Edmonton, before settling in the Victoria area in 2006. She is a full-time author whose work is inspired by a lifelong interest in social history, combined with a love of mystery. Smith has published over thirty books, most of which are collections of ghost stories inspired by true events, including *Campfire Stories of Western Canada*, *Ghostly Campfire Stories of Western Canada*, *Great Canadian Ghost Stories*, and perennial bestsellers *Ghost Stories of Alberta*, *Ghost Stories and Mysterious Creatures of British Columbia*, and *Ghost Stories of the Rocky Mountains*. She also appeared on the Discovery Channel's *Hunt for the Mad Trapper*. She lives in Sidney, BC.

MORE GREAT BOOKS FROM HERITAGE HOUSE

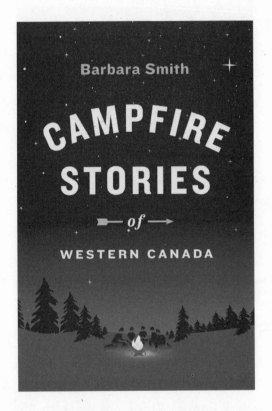

Campfire Stories of Western Canada

BARBARA SMITH

PRINT ISBN 978-1-77203-112-6

EBOOK ISBN 978-1-77203-113-3

Visit us at heritagehouse.ca

MORE GREAT BOOKS FROM HERITAGE HOUSE

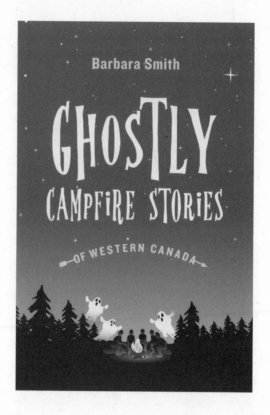

Ghostly Campfire Stories of Western Canada

BARBARA SMITH

PRINT ISBN 978-1-77203-245-1

EBOOK ISBN 978-1-77203-246-8

Visit us at heritagehouse.ca